ISBN-13:978-1493543946
ISBN-10: 1493543946

DEDICATION

My general opinion is that dedications should be made to people that believe in you and strive to give you confidence in your own abilities. Normally, those dedications are to living individuals. I will transcend that event and dedicate this to my mother. Lida Hooper Robbins passed from this life in 1992. She was 84 years old. She was the strongest woman I've ever known. She birthed 17 full term babies and raised 11 of them to adulthood, of which I'm the baby. My memories of her spurred me on many times in those moments that many writers get when they're not completely sure they'll ever be a published author. I hear, again, the words I heard many times while she was alive...'You can do anything you set your mind to do.' The key was setting my mind. Although I've questioned the validity of this for some occupations I could've chosen, for some reason I think she would have pushed me to fight to realize my dream. Thank you, Mom.

I dedicate this, also, to the sister nearest to me in age. She was eight years my senior, yet I slept with her until she married and moved out. I got her in trouble constantly with my relentless talking. She now supports my vocalization in books by helping me with research and giving me pep talks. Thank you Violet Robbins Shults. Her talented husband, Wilburn, is my music person for the YouTube book trailers. Thanks!

To my great niece Meagan Rouse, you are my encourager, my English tutor, and friend extraordinaire. I could never do this without you.

Thank you Ginny Barnes for being a friend…for reading and encouraging. As someone once said, “A friend is not a big thing. It’s a million little things.”

Of course, thank you Sam for being there for me every step of the way. You are patient, kind, and encouraging. Your retirement has allowed you to give more time to me on a regular basis, and I love it.

ACKNOWLEDGMENTS

I know that there are places in the heart of a person that are held special in his/her memory or experiences. Every place is moderately unique in things that happen there, but some stand apart in the avenues of time. There are two that arrest a special place in my heart. It's Clifton, South Carolina and Cocke County, Tennessee. I have lived at neither, having spent most of my years in middle Tennessee. My grandparents, whom I never knew, spent an unknown amount of time in Cocke County and three years in Clifton. My grandfather, and at least three of their children ages 9-14, worked in either Mill One or Mill Two (or both) in Spartanburg County where Clifton is located. My grandmother stayed at home, had babies, and tended to sick children in the heavily populated mill town. They lost three children to death while at Clifton. The children in my story were not a duplication of their deaths. This is fiction, after all. However, all fiction comes from deep within the writer; sometimes from the depth of the heart, and, for others, a concoction of the imagination of the brain, but mostly a combination of both. However, the *Sorrow* that my grandmother and grandfather experienced in Clifton left a cavernous hole for my need of knowledge of how they lived. Who could imagine that a place 442 miles from where I was born, and the events in the lives of people that I never knew could affect me so deeply? Thank you to my grandparents for your strength of character in the face of horrific sorrow.

I also want the towns of Clifton and Newport to know that I often change a name of a cemetery or living area and use my fictional license for a dramatic effect. This is especially true in the case of the cemetery site as well as some streets in Clifton.

Sorrow

....THE SIGHTED SISTER

Chapter 1

October 1900

Lottie used her hands to shade her eyes at the sound of steady hoof beats that shattered the quiet of the country farm. She put her hands down and picked at the dirt under her nails. Lottie glanced nervously down the road. She wasn't expecting company. Hardly anyone came up the road that dead-ended at their house unless they were coming to see them or was lost. She bent backwards and stretched her aching back. She had worked in the field of potatoes all morning, digging and putting them in bushel baskets. Her tongue swiped the dust off her lips, and she used her apron to wipe away the dirt that had settled on her sweaty face. The horse and rider stopped at the front of the house in a swirl of dust. Lottie ran home as fast as she could with seven year old daughter, August, at her heels.

Just as quickly as the rider came, he was gone. No hellos. No goodbyes. He handed her a paper, stained with sweat and smelling of dirt and body odor. Her hands shook as she unfolded it.

The thought of getting a telegram wrenched Lottie's stomach up in knots and brought on a sick feeling. She had never received a telegram before, but had lived with a sense of dread should one come. Her Mama had gotten one two years ago, right before her and the children left Jackson County, North Carolina. It had informed their family that Asa, her older brother, had been killed in a fall from a train trestle just north of Asheville.

She read to herself. *"Owen dead (stop) Do right with Beck (stop)"*

It was signed, *"Papa".*

The paper shook in the breeze as she reread the message. She plopped down on the porch and leaned her back against a post. Lottie's lips quivered and she threw her apron over her head and squalled. The paper fluttered to the ground.

"Mama, what's wrong?" August took her Mama's arm and shook it. She tugged at the apron and tried to pull it off her Mama's face.

In the distance, nine year-old Annie May dropped her basket of sweet potatoes and ran across the field to Lottie and August. "What's wrong? Who was that, Mama? What did he want?"

Lottie didn't answer. Annie picked up the paper and read it. Tears puddled in her eyes and made lines of mud down her dirty face.

"Annie May, what does it say?" August tried to grab the paper from her sister's hands.

Annie May twisted away from her sister. "It says our papa is dead?" She looked at her Mama's shaking body. "Is it true? Is Papa dead?" She bent down beside Lottie and pulled at her arm.

Lottie removed the stained apron from her face and used it to wipe the tears that ran down her face and had dripped a brownish-red on her dress. She stood up and stared toward the east, the direction of where they had lived in North Carolina. "I reckon he is. Now get yourself back out there. Pick up the rest of those sweet potatoes from the field and get 'em in the cellar. There's dampness in the air. We're due a rain. The land owner is expecting his part tomorrow. We can't be late getting them to him."

"How did Papa die?" August commenced to cry. "Was he sick? Why didn't somebody tell us?"

"The telegram didn't say. Now y'all get back out there and help your brothers in the field. I'll be along shortly."

"Let me stay here and go back with you," August begged.

Lottie pointed toward the field. "Get yourself out there."

Annie May and August did as they were told. It wouldn't be wise to do otherwise, not even with their papa dead somewhere.

August kicked at a clod of dirt. It sent a swirl of dust upward, and it blew back in their faces. Their tears were now mud. “Do you think Mama will take us to Papa’s funeral?”

“I don’t think she will. She told us a long time ago to forget about him. She said that Beck was our papa now, and we just needed to get used to it.”

August stopped and put her hands on her hips. “I call Beck Papa when I’m here at home, but I told my teacher at school that I wasn’t really a Radford and Beck was not my Papa. I told her my last name was Thompson.”

“You shouldn’t oughta done that, August. Mama would be mad if she knew. What made you do that?”

August looked away and bit her dirty fingernails. She turned around and put her hands on her hips. “Well, I AM a Thompson. The teacher looked at me real queer when I said it. You’re a Thompson, too. All of us are. They can call us whatever name they want to, but it don’t make it so.”

“Not anymore we won’t be a Thompson. Not if Mama marries Beck. I mean Papa.” She picked up a rock and threw it at the bushel basket of potatoes. “All this name changing makes my head feel all swimmy. I go by Radford like Mama told me to, and I guess I always will. But, like you said, my blood *is* Thompson blood.”

August knew it was best to get to work, but there was one more thing that bothered her. “Mama said one time that it didn’t matter what blood we carried, we were all Radford children to this world and to her. Can her marrying Beck make us have Radford blood?"

Annie May looked across the field and saw their Mama put her hands above her eyes and watch to see if they had obeyed.

"I don't want to talk about this anymore. Let's just hurry up and get finished so we can go to the house, else we are going to get our hide tanned."

Two year-old Sheffield was asleep under a tree at the end of the field. Eleven year-old Brody was digging the last potato hill at the end of his row. He stood up and yelled to the girls, "Who was that up there with Mama? What did he want?"

"If you wanted to know, you should've come up there with us. So, I ain't telling." Annie May looked at the dark clouds hanging above the tree line toward the west. A faint glow of lightning flashed within the cloud.

August stuck out her tongue at Annie May and yelled back to Brody. "It was a telegram man. He brought Mama a paper that said our Papa was dead."

Each girl took a side of the bushel basket and carried it to the end of the row where Brody knelt.

"So Papa is dead." Brody continued to dig. He acted like the news wasn't important. He was the oldest and probably remembered his Papa more than the others.

"That's what the paper had on it," Annie May said. "I read the wire."

August piped up. “The last letter we got from Grandpa said that Grandma was doing poorly. You don’t’ think she’ll die too, do you?”

“Maw-Maw will be fine. But as for Papa, well, that’s that, I guess. He won’t be hitting Mama no more or beating on me.”

August narrowed her eyes and poked a finger in Brody’s shoulder. “He never beat you. You’re just saying that because I didn’t tell you what the wire said. You’re making up lies.”

“You forget awfully easy, sister, or else he never hurt you as much as he did me or Mama. Maybe you were in the house when I was working in the fields and got beat with the plow lines for not keeping the row straight. It’s sad that he had to die, but I can’t say that I’m really sorry.”

“You’re hateful, Broadus Thompson.”

“I ain’t no Thompson. I’m a Radford. Don’t you know our last name? Maybe Mama needs to have that talk with you again.”

***

Lottie knew she was needed back in the fields to work, but she couldn’t bring herself to go back out there. There would be too many questions to answer from the children. Instead, she chose to sit on the edge of the porch and think about the telegram. She needed to tell Beck as quickly as she could.

Sorrow

There was no sorrow on her part for Owen's death, unless it was for his parents that lost a son. She always believed that he'd die young for his mean ways, but she couldn't stay around long enough for that to happen. That's why she let Beck take her away from her beloved North Carolina Mountains. She was afraid for her life and the children's. Nothing else could have made her leave.

She didn't aptly know what to call Beck as to their kinship, if you could call it that. A year ago, a woman at the General Store in Cosby had asked her if Beck was her husband. It was true what she said then. "Some things are just nobody's business." Last June, the census taker had asked her if he was her husband. Her answer, *cousin*, had sounded a little harsher than she had intended. It had also come out of her mouth before she had taken the time to think about it. He wasn't her cousin at all. They weren't even blood kin.

Once again dust churned into a cloud down the road, but it came at a slower pace than earlier. It was Beck. Lottie thought about how she should tell him about Owen. He had protected her from her husband for months before they had left Jackson County, North Carolina, leaving only after Owen had almost killed her and the baby that she was carrying, which was Sheffield.

August left the field and ran to the house when she saw dust. "Papa is dead." She told Beck before her Mama could speak.

Beck stood by the horse with his hands on the saddle. He did not turn around but untied the leather string and took off his saddle bags. "Get back to the field and help your brothers and sister, August Radford. Do it right now."

Beck turned and looked at Lottie's tear-stained face. "Get in the house, Lottie. Wash your face and get dressed. We're going to Newport. It's time we got married."

***

Lottie watched Beck as he and Ed Burnett signed the marriage papers and wrote in the date, October 11, 1900. Ed was Beck's boss on the farm and agreed to sign as a surety for the marriage license. Each of the men shook hands with John Susong, the Justice of the Peace. She was now legally Mrs. Beckley Radford, not that it wasn't time.

She thought about how they came to be in Tennessee. It was during the worst times she had with her first husband, Owen. Beck had brought them to the part of the country where he had been born, and they had lived in Tennessee ever since. First in Sevier County, but Owen had found them. They were living on a farm while Beck worked at the Stokely Brothers cannery on Seehorn Creek. Owen shot their cow. The sorry man knew it was the only way to have milk for the children, but he did it anyway. If she had any feeling that she might forget all Owen had done to her and her family, this caused her memory to recover.

They moved to Cosby for a time, but Owen found them once more. This time he lied and told the boss on the farm where they worked that Beck was a horse thief. They fired him. Beck being a thief was a lie. The horse in question was the one that Lottie's Papa had given her when she married, but Owen told them it was his horse, and that Beck had stolen it.

Always running. Living in sin. They couldn't marry and make things right like Papa wanted as she was still married to Owen. She couldn't divorce him or he would find where they lived again. He didn't take kindly to being made a fool of, he said. Not that she was making a fool of him, but he made it seem that way to everyone else. He acted like he hated her and the children, but he didn't want anyone else to have them, especially Beck.

They moved to Cocke County, near to the town of Newport, and worked on the farm where they now lived. There had been no other attempt to find them.

Beck had once said that Owen would be better off dead...that somebody ought to kill him and tell God he had died. She agreed but that didn't seem likely to happen. His family was business people in North Carolina, and everyone thought they could do no wrong. His daddy might have been an honorable man, but Owen was not.

Lottie was sure she and the children have been better off with Beck during the past two years, even if they weren't married. Beck never hit her, and he worked hard to make a living. She didn't know if he really loved her or if he just felt sorry for the lot of them.

Lottie longed to be a child again. She dreamed lately, both when she was asleep and when she was awake, about her Papa and Mama and how they had been so good to her. She thought about how she had wanted to fall in love. Childish dreams of love crumbled like the fall leaves under her feet. Grown up love was difficult.

The night before she met Owen, she had dreamed about death. That was a sure sign of a wedding, so her Mama had said. Maybe she should have just taken it to mean exactly what she dreamed, a death. She shouldn't have been so bent on marrying the first boy she had taken a liking to. In ways, all her life had felt like one death after another long before Owen passed.

Over a table in the magistrate's office, there hung a mirror. She walked over and peered at her reflection. When she was young, she had felt beautiful. Sassy as could be, with dreams of finding love and making a family. But now look at that woman, she thought. She rubbed her finger over her crooked nose, left from that last punch in the face by Owen. Her nose had oozed blood for two weeks. She had pushed rags up inside her nose each night to keep it from staining her pillow.

Lottie rubbed the scar on her upper lip. That happened the day Owen threw her across the room and against the wall. She'd been in the family way with Jacin. There'd been no time to mend from his death before she was in the family way with Sheffield. Jacin had been born in January and died quietly that same night. Sheffield had come in December of the same year.

She swallowed hard and tried to smile at herself in the mirror. Tears ran down her face in relief because her oppression was finally over. Thankfully, her sweet baby Jacin, and any other baby she had lost in death and was now in heaven, wouldn't ever have to see their daddy. Owen was surely burning in hell right now.

Chapter 2

Late October 1900

About two weeks before the wire came, Lottie had told Beck that she was in the family way. He took the news like the man that she knew he was. He told her that he was as much to blame as her, but that he would need to make more money than he did on this farm to support them. Instead of running from Owen, they now needed to move to feed their growing family.

The day after her announcement, he left to run an errand for his boss, traveling to Waynesville, North Carolina. She was so glad he had gotten home right after the telegram had come.

People were anxious for jobs, and it didn't take long for word to get around that there were mills operating on the Pacolet river just across the state line in South Carolina that were seeking workers. Beck left, along with a few other men from Newport, to try to get those jobs. He had been gone for five days.

Lottie didn't sleep well when Beck was not in the house. Last night she had tossed for an hour, and when she did sleep, she had dreamed. In the dream, a black buggy had come to the house where they lived. It was a much larger house than the one they now lived in on the farm. There were four rooms, and the house sat high upon a hill, on land without trees or grass. Beck and Lottie had sat on the porch of the house as a black buggy came out of the darkness, the traces of the harness rattling long before it appeared. A man came into the house and took a small casket to the buggy. It left and came back twice more, each time removing a tiny casket and taking it away. Lottie couldn't console Beck who had cried more over the second casket than the other two.

Annie May had awakened her Mama in the wee hours of the morning when her moaning and crying had scared all the children. Annie May had begged her to tell the dream, but Lottie couldn't bring herself to talk about it. It had felt so real. She didn't mention the dream to Beck when he came back to get them. She had a feeling this death dream did not mean a wedding this time, either.

Lottie thought about how her Papa and Mama had lived all their lives in the mountains and their parents before them had done the same. She was moving for the fifth time in her life. First was with Mama and Papa, and then she moved into hers and

Owen's house. Next was when she moved into the house with Beck, next to White Oak Flats in Sevier County, up to Cosby, then they moved to Newport with little more than the clothes on their back. The furniture they had accumulated was rough and handmade but serviceable. Now, she was off to another state, South Carolina. Beck had told her the mill would move them by train, and there would be a mill house provided where they would live. They would have to pay the company back for the move, a little money from each pay for a while, and the mill would also take out a small amount of rent for the house.

The children could not hold down their excitement. Beck's promise of another train ride and living in a town where friends would be nearby to play with made them jump and dance.

***

All their belongings were on the wagon, and it was time to head to the train station. They would pack it on a box car which would take them to Spartanburg, South Carolina. There, they would rent a wagon, drive it to Clifton, and find the house Beck had been given that was near the mill. He tried to describe how the town looked, but she couldn't get her heart to be as excited about it as he was.

Beck pulled the wagon near to the tracks. Families sat on piles of their belongings and waited for the train. Lottie laid her hand on Beck's arm.

"Can't we go see Mama and Papa in Jackson County before we go?"

Beck looked at Lottie. "I told you we can't. We best be taking our family and getting on with our lives. This job is important. I don't want them giving it to anybody else."

"But, Beck, Papa and Mama are getting old. It might be too late. Papa says Mama is not well at all and..."

With one hand, Beck held the reins and, with the other, reached out and took Lottie's hand. She looked at him with tears in her eyes.

He wrinkled his forehead. "All my life, all I've ever seen is hard times. It's tough to make a living on a farm that's not your own. I tried working on the road and logging, and I lost my family. No matter what I did, it just wasn't enough. It feels the same way now. The house we just left had cracks so big in the floor that you can see the chickens between the boards. Rats came in and snakes. When I was in Clifton, I saw families all working in the mills together. It wasn't easy work but, with all them doing their part, they had to be doing well. The houses were serviceable. The boards on the floor met, and you could not see the ground below.

"In the mill, whole families worked together... boys and girls Brody's and Annie May's age. We could put all our money together and buy a nice house. They took us through the mill, and I saw men that were bosses. I know they made the best money, because they were dressed better than the others.

People did what they said. It might be that I can get a job like that. The children will live in a town. There's a school and a teacher. Churches of all kinds are there."

"But how can Brody or Annie May go to school if you want them to work in the mill?"

Beck pulled his hand away from Lottie. "They wouldn't have to work all the time I don't reckon. If they have a school building, the children must surely get some learning in. Maybe they change out the children that work from time to time. Brody would make a fine worker."

Lottie wiped her tears. "If you think that's what we need to do, then we will. I just wanted to see Mama and Papa so bad."

"You can write to them, every day if you want. Send it right through the mail like everyone else. They have a post office just under the hill from our house. It'll be just like you're there. You'll hear all about their lives, and they'll hear all about yours."

"That's not the same as seeing their faces." Lottie closed her eyes tight and tried to picture her Papa's face. It was hard.

Beck drew in a deep breath and blew it out. "If we all work hard, maybe we can send them the money so they can ride the train out there and see us."

Lottie's eyes grew large. "Could we really do that? Do you think they'd come?"

"I guess you'll just have to write and ask them."

***

Beck and a hired man unloaded the wagon, and Beck left to deliver both horse and wagon to the blacksmith shop in Newport. Someone had said they would meet him there and buy it.

Lottie looked at their pile of things on the planks by the train tracks. These were all the belongings they owned in the world.

"Annie May, stay here and watch out for your brothers and sisters. I'll be back real soon."

"Where are you going?"

"You don't pay any mind to where I'm going. You just do as I say."

"I wanna go." August begged.

"All of you stay here. Stay together, and mind your own business."

The telegraph office was down the street, and she hurried to send a wire.

Did right with Beck (stop) Moving Clifton SC (stop) Will send letter (stop) Lottie

Lottie reached in her hand and untied her mom's handkerchief from the undergarment beneath the bosom of her dress. Tied up in one corner was egg money she had saved for a time that she felt she would really need it. This was that time. It cost all that she had except for one nickel. She tied the nickel back inside the corner of the handkerchief and put it back in her underclothes.

Uneasiness had hung on her ever since Beck had come back, and they had married. He didn't seem surprised at all of the death of Owen. Just matter-of-fact told her to get dressed...that they were getting married. She wished August had not come running up that day. She wanted to ask if he had already known.

She felt jittery inside. She could ask him, but she might not want to hear the answer. They had talked many days about when they could marry. Both knew it would not be until Owen died, and now he was out of the way.

She heard the train whistle in the distance and hurried back to the station. The children were nowhere near the pile of their belongings. In fact, they were nowhere to be found.

She searched. There was a crowd that had gathered around an automobile. She could only see the front portion due to the crowd. People stood on every side, some holding their horses and others grabbed their children. They all wanted to look at the first one of its kind seen in Cocke County. The papers advertised them, and it wouldn't be long until the rich land owners would buy their own. It was peculiar looking. It didn't draw her interest at all. She figured they'd never own an automobile, and so she had no need to see one.

She moved through the crowd and finally found Brody standing on a contraption on the side of the automobile and leaning over the door. He jerked a round-shaped thing back and forth. Annie jumped up beside him. She reached over and hit something. The car made a terrible racket.

"Listen to that horn. Ain't that a fine piece of work," a man near her yelled.

Lottie ran to them and grabbed an arm of each child. She pulled them to the edge of the crowd where August held Sheffield in her arms. Beck came and herded the children back toward the station just as the train pulled in. This was as exciting to them as the automobile. Their second train ride.

The trip would have held eagerness for her too if it were not for a feeling of dread and fear that lingered from her dream. When would it happen? It would, she was sure of that. She was blessed to be able to foretell the future with her dreams...the sighted sister. Her Mama said that the peculiar gift came from her grandmother's side of the family, and it was both a blessing and a curse. She longed for the day it would be a blessing. It had only been a curse up until now.

Chapter 3

November 1900

Lottie's heart sank. "I can't move in here." She stared at the house, as she noted the front porch she remembered from her dream.

Beck stared at her and then at the children. He grabbed Lottie by the arm and pulled her to the edge of the steps. "What do you mean? We have to move in this house. It's the one they gave us. The house is larger than any wherever we've lived. The boys will have their room and the girls the other. We will even have a bedroom of our own. There are four rooms. It only costs us fifty cents a month for each room. That's plum reasonable. It'll make life a lot easier for all of us."

"It ain't about the size. This house was in a dream I dreamt whilst you came here to get the work. There's death in this house."

Lottie knew Beck couldn't understand how a dream could matter. She shouldn't tell him yet, but she needed to. All her mama's threats and stories of how telling a dream within a week of having it would make it come true kept her quiet. She couldn't bring herself to speak it out loud.

"Come on. Don't act like this. I need this job. I've got to have it to feed this family. I didn't put you down to work, what with you expecting a baby, but Brody will be a good worker."

"Brody's just a boy. Do they hire eleven year old boys to work?"

"I told you. They said a right smart of young boys are working, some as young as six. I saw dozens with my own eyes. Girls, too. Whole families came to the mill together."

Lottie bit her lip, and tears came to her eyes. "I guess I don't have a choice but to move in. But there's sorrow here, for all of us. This place has a black cover all around it."

"Set up housekeeping, and meet some neighbors. You'll feel better then. That black cloud is just stuff your Mama filled your head with. It ain't true. Tell me the dream."

"I ain't telling, at least not until next week."

Beck sighed.

Lottie watched Beck pull the crates off the wagon and carry them inside. There was nothing left for her to do but unpack.

The children jumped to the ground and ran toward the road. "Annie May. Stay here and help me."

"Mama. Can't I meet some people and see if I can find a friend?"

"Not till all this is put away."

Annie May came back and took a crate into the house.

Lottie stopped on the porch. "What's that other door that comes out on the porch? Do we have two front doors?" Lottie asked Beck.

"There's another family living in there. I ain't met them, but I heard children playing in there when I was here last week."

Lottie's face flushed, and she set down her crate. "Another family? What kind of house has two families that don't even know each other living under the same roof?"

Beck rubbed his neck. "All the houses are like that. There are walls between us. You can't go from their part to ours except'n you come outside and knock on each other's door."

"That's crazy...to be under the same roof like that. Lordy, they can hear everything we say, and us them. Why would anyone build a house like that?" Lottie eyes narrowed. "Why didn't you tell me this? This is not right. Strangers don't live in a house together."

"I don't know, but we don't live together. We live side by side but without any land between us. Come on, and let's get moved in."

"That's plum crazy. No land in between us! Hmph!" Lottie traipsed through the house and stood at the back door. She looked at small wooden buildings in a row at the back of each house.

Beck leaned over her shoulder. "Those are the outhouses. Each house has one."

"Hmph. Do we have to share that too?" She snapped at him.

"There's a chicken house, too. The people that lived on our side of the house before us built it from scrap lumber they found near the river, and the superintendent said we could use it. I'll try to find a place where we can buy a few chickens. Right now, I need your help. I have to be at work before daylight in the morning, starting day after tomorrow. Everyone says the mill blows a whistle which signals getting-up-time one hour before the second whistle that will sound to begin work. I can't be late. The day we came from Newport, some of the men at the store told us that if you are late two days, you lost the job. If it was daylight, I'd wake up on my own, but we start an hour before daylight. Once I get used to waking up, I'll do it on my own. The children will learn to get up before daylight too. I can bring one of the children to start the second day after me."

"One of the children? I thought Brody was the only one going to work." Lottie drew her eyebrows together at the thought of any of the other babies toiling away at the mill.

"Annie May has a job, too. There are girls working younger than her."

She was already too tired to argue with him. The wagon was borrowed so they needed to unload and get it back to its owner. Beck would come back by and sign up the workers at the mill.

Lottie's legs felt heavy as she walked up the steps. The house was in good repair, but she knew for sure it was the one that had been in her dream...the one with the black buggy. Death.

Lottie stopped at the door, set her crate down, and looked up. "Oh God. I don't know if You can change this, but I'm here a-asking you to do just that. Don't let death come near our door." She whispered under her breath. She made a cross in the air with her finger. Lottie picked up her crate and used her shoulder to push open the door.

***

Beck turned in his first month's rent and signed up the ones that would be working from the family. Everything was ready for their new start.

He walked back over the bridge toward the house. He stopped and watched the water flow under the bridge and over the dam. Below the dam, there were huge rocks that stuck up out of the water. One was at least ten feet wide and flat on top. It was easily accessed from the land, and Beck went down and climbed on it. He could see the mill, much of the village, and down the river. He laid back and rested in the sun.

When he came to Clifton with the others looking for work, a man with a high position at the mill took them outside and talked about the area and how much they would enjoy the close-knit family life of the town.

The Pacolet River was made up of the North Fork and the South Fork. They each run about 50 miles in the northwestern part of the state. The two forks join north of Spartanburg about 10 miles, then flow around the outer edges of Spartanburg County and two other counties, Cherokee and Union County. It finally joins the Broad River past the town of Pacolet.

Beck had caught sight of the river as they either went across or near it while they were on the train. It was almost as pretty as the Tuckasegee in Jackson County. He knew that if Lottie would get out and explore the area, she would feel the same toward her new home as she did her old one. She loved trees, and the banks were covered with sycamore, oaks, and river birch. He had seen red maple and even mountain laurel. Maybe these would make up for the lack of trees on the hillside. Those had been used for lumber for the houses where they now lived.

A turtle popped his head up at the base of the rock. Downstream a beaver jumped into the water and swam across.

During the next hour, he noticed kingfishers and herons. If he could imagine all the houses gone and the trees back in their place, it would be like being in the mountains.

This might be the last time he would have a quiet moment to himself. The day after tomorrow, he had to be at work. Even now, he could hear the hum and clanking from the mill's open windows above him. The main complaints he had heard was the dust from the cotton and the endless noise. The mill ran six days a week with two twelve hour shifts each day.

The warm sunshine made him sleepy, and he leaned back and laid on the rock. He dreamed of his papa and mama. On his arm was his first gun, and Papa had his hand on his shoulder. He stooped down and pulled Beck to face him. "Life is not always what you expect, boy. Sometimes, you have to take what it gives and build on it."

A horse clomped across the bridge and woke him. It was time to get back to Lottie, but he felt sad as he remembered his father's face staring at him during the dream.

***

Not until she decided to start supper did Lottie realize she had no idea where to get water.

"Beck, where do we get water? Do we need to walk all the way to the river and scoop it up into a bucket?"

Beck laughed. "No. Let me show you." He took her and Annie May to the back of the house and walked with them past two houses. There stood a hand pump. "We are closer than some to the water. There are wells scattered over the hillside with pumps like this. You can send one of the children down here whenever you need water from the well."

"A well. My grandma had one of those. But Papa always had a spring nearby where we got water. It always tasted fresh."

"This water tastes good. Here's a jar of water beside the pump. Make sure you leave it full for the next person. It's to prime the pump to get water started coming out. Like this." He pulled up the handle and then pushed it down while pouring water into a space that sent water down the pipe. Soon water flowed fast into the bucket they had brought with them. "If all else fails, you can pull the top of the well off and use the rope and bucket."

"We better learn to share, don't you guess? We share an outhouse with the family that lives under our roof and a well with who knows how many people. If you're very thirsty or have the backyard trots, it's just too bad if someone else beats you there."

"Oh Lottie!" Beck marched back to the house.

***

A clanging bell and voices brought Lottie away from clearing the table and rushed to the door. She moved to the side when Beck reached for the door.

"That's a thing called a trolley. We can ride it to work. For the time being, I'll walk. Not yet sure how it all works. Just be careful, I don't think it could stop if you didn't get out of the way. It might run right over you."

Beck looked at Lottie's eyes, large and dark with fear. "It'll be fun living in town. You wait and see. We'll make friends, and the children will have a right smart of young people to play with. It may take some getting used to, but I honestly believe you'll like it before long."

"You think so...hmmm. Don't count your chickens yet."

***

Lottie laid the hammer down and hung coats, as tattered as they were, on nails. She put the children's low and hers and Beck's higher. All the clothes had been put away. An old skirt hung over the window of her bedroom. She made another curtain by hanging one apron high and another below it to cover the window that looked out on the porch. She didn't want the people that lived on the other side of the house to come and peep in.

Beck had given her what little money they had left from their travel. He told her to go left at the road in front of their house and, at the end of the street, to turn right and go down the hill. She would see the company store beside the bridge. He said for her to get a few staples ...maybe some flour and meal, salt, and a little molasses, if she could afford it. If there was enough money, she planned to buy coffee as well. She left Annie May and Brody to watch August and Sheffield.

Lottie latched the back door and went out on the front porch. She looked at the houses over the hillside and thought about the mountains back home. The nights would already be right chilly in Jackson County. The days would be so beautiful with color that they could put a rainbow to shame. Last night, their second in Clifton, there had been a nip in the air like fall would soon be here, but today you couldn't tell it. There was no wind, and the temperature already had her sweating, unusual for November.

She turned and locked the front door. It was impossible not to worry about the other door, side-by-side to hers. Lottie stared at it. *Are they watching me leave?* At the thought, she looked at the window and saw a lace curtain fall. She waved and left with a smile.

Most of the houses lay quiet. No women were doing their washing or children moving around outside like she expected. Probably the entire family was at work in the mill like Beck had said. There was a woman and baby here and there. She nodded to them, and they nodded back. The "trolley" had not passed again since early that morning.

The store stood on the bank of the Pacolet River, across the bridge and to the left. The bridge stretched over the still waters right before they fell over the dam. Below the wall, the water rushed around large rocks. The mill stood on the hill above the dam. She saw women sitting at large machines. They raised and lowered their arms as they worked. She saw a man walk by the window and stop at one, then another of the machines. Once in a while, a little boy would run down the length of the mill. He came back slower, stopped, and handed something to each worker.

She waited for a wagon to cross and then stepped onto the bridge. She carefully walked on the part made for wagon wheels of the wagons. There were missing boards and you could see the water below. She thought about how horrible it would be to fall into the water. Lottie had never learned to swim. Her mother's thoughts had been, "you can go down to the creek as soon as you learn to swim," so she never learned. She was glad that Beck had taught her children to swim in the waters of the French Broad River in Tennessee. It was a horrible feeling to be scared of the water, and she didn't want her children to have her same fears.

The gaps in boards were small but she pictured her foot catching in the crack and throwing her into the waters below. She held her breath. About half-way, Lottie ran. She made the longest steps possible and tried to not look down.

Lottie climbed the steps. She stood on the store porch which wrapped around two sides of the building. There were straight backed chairs in a row across the front. She looked in the front window and noted its finery. She had never seen a store window with such fine things to sell in it, all fixed up so pretty. It had the most beautiful dress she had ever seen. It hung on a wood frame. Above it, hanging from a string, was a pretty hat. She had seen one like it in a catalog while she was Tennessee. It was fancier in person. Right beside the dress, on a table, was a pair of shoes. They had tiny buttons and little loops that went over the buttons from the toes to the top of the little boots. On the other side of the dress was a man's fine coat and breeches. "Oh my, Beck would look so handsome in that there suit."

"Can I help you, ma'am? Did you say you want to see that suit? Come on inside, and I'll show it to you."

Bright red color slid across Lottie's face and disappeared down the neck of her dress. "No. Don't think I'm interested right now." She swallowed hard and looked past the storekeeper and into the open door. "I may need to get a few things, though. That is if I can come inside and look."

"Of course you can come in. I'm pretty sure we'll have whatever you need. If not, I can get it for you out of Spartanburg, although some things may have to come by train from Asheville or Greenville."

Inside the door were stacks of kindling wood and buckets of coal. She had noticed big piles of each outside on the other side of the store.

Lottie walked up and down the four passages between shelves that were head high. There was hoop cheese, a barrel of molasses, loose salt, sugar, and something they called salt mackerel. Plugs of tobacco hung over the table where the storekeeper stood. Behind him were medicines and remedies. She saw camphorated oil, catnip tea, castor oil, and Epsom salts. Little glass containers below the medicines were filled with seeds.

Under a table sat flour in cloth sacks. One end of the table held yard goods in every color she could image.

One whole row had all kinds of hardware. Lottie made a fist and bit hard on her folded fingers as she looked at a hundred or so casket handles and hinges. She knew that was what they were because there was a child's casket beside them with hardware already added. It had brass corner knobs. Lottie reached out and raised the cover. Chills ran down her spine when she ran her fingers over the soft blue material that lined the casket. She shut the top and backed away.

The last row had baby clothes. Past them were all different sizes of clothes for children. On the back side of that row were dresses and fancy underclothes for women. Suits hung on a rack along with winter coats for both men and women.

She took one sweeping look around the entire store. *Everything from cradle to the grave*, she thought.

"So, are you new to the area?" The man looked at her from head to toe.

Lottie nodded.

"I thought so. How long have you been here?"

"We came on the train the day before yesterday." Lottie stood in front of the counter and looked at the jars of candy. Her mouth watered like a child at the thought of the sweets. "I need a few things."

"Tell me what you need, and I'll help. You might want to make note of the Clifton address. Give it to your family back home. This is your post office, and you can pick up mail any time after noon most every day. I have postage stamps, paper, and envelopes."

The storekeeper continued. "I don't know if you know it or not, but part of your pay will be issued in coupon books that will have money marks in them, 25 cents, 10 cents, 5 cents, 2 cents, and 1 cent. It'll trade just like money here at the store." He showed her a page from someone's book.

Lottie read on the front of the coupon ***Payable Only in Merchandise***. "What happens if you need money instead?"

The man shrugged his shoulders. "You'd have to ask a company man. Sometimes they'll let you have an advance on the pay if it's a real emergency. They hardly ever do it, though."

She left with the items from her list except for the coffee. There hadn't been enough money. She was glad she hadn't asked him to measure any out. She would've felt awful if she had to make him put it back.

Chapter 4

November 1900

The week passed quickly. Beck had taken Brody in and got him set up with a job. Brody slept fitfully the night after his first day at work, crying out in his sleep. When Lottie asked the next morning what he had dreamed, he told her he had worked his job in dreams all night long.

Beck laughed. "Too bad you didn't get paid for that shift, too."

Lottie felt sorry for her young son that was so worried about failing to do a good job that it had plagued him all night. He moaned in his sleep for a whole week.

A few days after Brody went to work, Annie May started. She didn't dream like Brody, but she was quieter than usual the second morning.

"What's wrong, Annie girl? You're awfully quiet this morning." Lottie spun Annie May's hair in a twist and put it up on her head. She poked in hair pins to secure it. It was then she noticed the tears streaming down Annie May's face.

"Oh, Mama, I don't know if I can learn to do that job. There are so many things to remember. I hear them yelling at other girls when they make a miss-lick. What if I mess up and it causes the line to shut down? The bosses hate it."

Lottie teared up. "I don't know nothing about lines or whatever you are talking about, but I know that if anyone else can do a job, then you can too. You're a smart girl. Just make sure you understand what they're saying you should do. If you don't understand, then tell them to repeat it until you do know what they're saying. You'll do just fine. In fact, you look smarter than any girl I've seen pass this house on her way to work."

Annie May laughed and dried her tears. "I don't think it has anything to do with looks, Mama. But, you're right. I can do anything they can do."

"That's right, baby girl. You show them that." Lottie hugged her daughter tight. Tomorrow Annie May would turn ten years old. She wasn't a little girl any longer. "Don't forget that lunch pail."

Lottie stood at the door as her family left for work. She leaned against the wall and wished she and her family was in the beautiful mountains of North Carolina, far away from crowds and close neighbors.

***

Beck waited until after supper and the children were in bed to talk to Lottie. He had felt dread all day about the whole situation. She was washing dishes.

"In the morning, you need to get August up with the rest of us. I have to take her in to work with me."

Lottie dried her hands on her apron and turned to him. "No! I will not. She's just a baby. She turned eight only a week ago."

"We have a four room house. That means we have to have four people working. There are jobs that she can do that ain't too hard. I wish that Brody had started as a sweeper instead of a doffer. They say the superintendent of the mill started out as a sweeper. Both boy and girls can sweep. She might be a sweeper or something else that's easy work."

"It's the *'or something else'* that worries me! You said some of the jobs there are dangerous. How could you think about letting her work?"

Beck leaned against the table. "I didn't have a choice. I wanted a four room house. Now, I'm beholden to them to supply four workers."

"Then I'll work." Lottie put her hands on her hips.

"Stop it, Lottie. You have Sheffield to tend to, and you can't take him with you. You're also in the family way, and need to be at home. I'll check on August every time I can."

"I want to go home to the mountains. I hate this place."

Beck walked to the door of their bedroom and opened it a smite. “If we lived on a farm, she’d be planting potatoes, chopping corn, shucking corn, and feeding the farm animals…just like we all did as children. You name the job, she’d be helping. What’s the difference?”

Lottie began to cry. “I don’t know how it’s different, but it is. It seems wrong somehow for a baby to be working in a factory.”

“It’s no different. Have her ready to leave with the rest of us.”

Lottie walked in front of him. “I see women in the family way walk by every day on the way to work in the mill. Some have a baby by the hand that they’re taking with them. Who keeps those babies?”

I don’t know. They may be going to the store and not to work.”

“Well, they sure stay a long time at the store. They don’t come home for twelve hours just like the rest of you.”

“Leave it be, Lottie. I want you here with Sheffield. Our baby will be here before we know it.”

Beck went to bed. Lottie sat down at the table and cried. She was still there when the rooster crowed the next morning and the getting-up whistle blew.

***

Lottie pulled Annie May's hair back and put it behind her ear. She picked at the lint scattered through her daughter's dark locks.

"What's it like working in the mill? Is it hard?"

Annie May shook her head. "Not really hard. Now that I know what to do, it seems pretty easy. Down right boring at times. I daydream a lot."

Lottie brushed Annie May's hair. "Daydream? What about?"

"About what it was like in the mountains, and pretend I'm talking to my friends from there and telling them about my life now. I wonder about who I'll marry and where I'll live. I'm afraid I might have to move away from you like you have from Grandpa. That would be awful."

Lottie put down the brush. "I hope that never happens. You need to be close to your Mama."

"I guess it depends on what my man wants, if I ever get one. Anyway, that gets terribly sad, so I talk to the women around me. The good part is that we're like family. I know everybody and what's happening in their life. It didn't take me much time at all until I knew almost everything about everybody. No one told me it'd be like that. We're family. We take up for each other and cover for each other if someone has to go to the outhouse."

"You have family here in this house. The other workers are not your family. I should be working at the mill instead of you. Maybe we could swap…me at the mill and you here with the babies."

"I can't birth that baby you're carrying." Annie May laughed. "I guess you best do as Papa says and stay home. There are women there that are in the family way. One has her older daughter, that's maybe seven or eight years old, bring the baby by so the mama can nurse a few times a day. The foreman frowns on it but, because everyone gives him the evil eye, he pretends he don't see it."

"Do you think they would hire me even though the baby is due in a couple of months?" Lottie bit her lip.

"I don't know, but I don't think Beck...I mean Papa...would let you work. Do you?"

Lottie crossed her arms and tapped her toe. "I don't know why he's so hard against me going to work in the mill. We could make more money. In no time, we could move away and buy us a farm, or go back home to the mountains."

Annie looked down at Sheffield and back at her Mama's huge belly. "He's probably right having you stay here. The women that work come into the mill dead tired. They say they don't get to bed until midnight, and they're back up at 4:00 a.m. cooking and cleaning so they can come back to the mill. Their babies run wild all over town. Last week, one of them fell into an outhouse hole and died. Even I'd rather you stay at home."

It was strange to Lottie that she and Annie May talked like two women instead of mother and daughter. Her children had grown up since they came to town.

***

Annie May motioned to one of the little girls that sat with the other children, all about 7 to 8 years of age, near the middle of the long room. There were boxes at the doffers' feet, and they kept an eye out for spinners that needed empty bobbins. It was too loud to hear anyone call out, so they watched for hand signals from the spinner girls. Most of them ran out of bobbins about the same time, so the children only worked about fifteen to twenty minutes an hour. The rest of the time, they would look at their ABC books or knit stockings and mittens. The group changed from day to day as children came down with the fever and went home sick. Others would sometimes be told to go to school the next day. As soon as the foreman knew there were not enough bobbin children to work, he'd send up to the schoolhouse and ask that the teacher bring down however many that was needed to keep up production.

"Hold up two fingers so she'll bring another girl with her," Lizzie yelled at Annie May.

Lizzie was four years older than Annie, but they were good friends.

Bobbins in hand, they went back to business. Spinning had become automatic to both girls, and they could talk and do the work. Because of the noise, the women yelled back and forth, and there was nothing secret in the spinning room.

"That boy we met last Sunday asked me to meet him down at the River. I want you to come with me." Lizzie raised her eyebrows as she waited for Annie May's answer.

"He's awfully old for you, don't you think?" Annie didn't like him. She had seen him lose his temper with someone last week and pick a fight. He hit a boy that was a good five years younger than himself. This didn't seem to bother Lizzie, but it did her. If he did that to a younger child, what would he do to Lizzie if, God forbid, he got mad at her.

"No, not too old at all. Girls tend to marry young in Clifton, and to men of a greater age than themselves. The older men have worked awhile, and they usually have a little money saved up. That could come in handy, don't you think?"

Annie May licked her fingers and twisted the two ends of cotton together and continued spinning. "I think money don't mean a thing if you're not happy. Buying things does not mean a person will treat you right, and I don't think that man will be good to you."

"So what does being good to a woman mean to you? Would it be not to have to work in the mill? Having a house of your own that nobody can make you move? What?"

Annie wrinkled her forehead and waited. "I don't mind working in the mill, but I want him to be even tempered. I've seen men hit their women. I don't plan on ever letting a man hurt me. It seems risky marrying a man too many years older than yourself."

"You're only ten years old...really just a child."

Annie May stuck out her tongue at Lizzie. "You're only 14...not much older."

"Four years between us is not the same as four years between a boy and a girl to you?" Lizzie asked.

"It's not the same." Annie May yelled.

"It is too the same thing. Anyway, I'm almost 15. A good deal of girls is married at 13 or 14 years old. I fear I'll end up being an old maid if I don't' marry soon."

"You'll be sorry." Annie frowned.

Lizzie thought it best to change the subject. "I heard someone say they might move me to the weave room. If they do, I'll try to get you on there. It's more money."

She and Lizzie continued to spin.

Chapter 5

November 1900

Lottie took her apron and wiped the sweat from her face. It was too hot to cook, but what else could she do? Everybody had to eat. They'd want cornbread with the beans she'd cooked early this morning. She pulled the bread from the oven and set it on the top of the stove. Sunday might be a day of rest for the mill but not for a wife and mother.

"Annie May, set the table."

All the food was ready to eat anytime Beck got home from wherever he had wandered off to this Sunday.

The wind blew Lottie's damp hair when she stepped out on the porch. The sun had set and a light breeze was just what she needed.

"The leaves will never change if it don't get cooler than this. The seasons are out of whack, nothing like what we have in the mountains," she said to no one in particular.

Lottie picked up the axe that Beck had used to chop up kindling for the cookstove last night. Lottie sat down on the step and leaned the axe against the porch post beside her. She watched August and Sheffield play in the dirt at the bottom of the steps. A little girl of about three years old sat with them.

A door slammed behind her. She glanced back and watched the neighbor from the other side of the house lean back against the door. She turned back to watch the children.

"You're not a friendly bunch are you?" The neighbor asked loudly.

Lottie bit her lip. "Where I come from, the people that already live in the area, they's the ones that come to the newcomers." Lottie tapped her toe on the step below her, and squeezed her hands into fists and pushed them between her legs.

"Is that right? I didn't know you had neighbors in the mountains. I thought you all lived…"

The little girl sitting beside Lottie's children in the dirt let out a scream like she was dying. Lottie looked just in time to see Sheffield drop her arm. There were teeth marks about half way between her wrist and elbow.

Before Lottie could get up, the woman jumped from the top step and landed beside her daughter. She grabbed her child's arm and looked at the teeth marks. She turned to Sheffield and grabbed him by the shoulders and jerked him up. His teeth rattled as she shook him. "You little half-breed, what do you think you're doing?" She stood his feet on the ground and pushed him backward. Sheffield fell in the dirt.

Lottie slid down a step and motioned for Sheffield to run to her. The woman swung around and faced Sheffield and Lottie. Her face was red and her eyes two balls of fire. "Keep your half-breed children away from my child. Back-wood crazy people are what you are."

"My children ain't half-breeds."

"Is that right? I see their dark hair that you keep plaited, pulled back from their face like an Indian child. She looked at August with her braided hair. You may think we can't tell a half breed, but everyone here can see the truth. That dark skin. Hmph. You can't hide your Indian blood. It comes out in the children. As your husband ain't dark, I'm thinking there might be a surprise in the woodpile."

Lottie put her hands behind her to push herself up, and her fingers touched the axe. *Nobody calls my children half-breeds.* With one swoop, she leapt to her feet and brought the axe around in front of her. She grabbed the woman by the hair of the head. Lottie drug her to the edge of the porch and pushed her head down. She raised the axe.

A strong hand grabbed her wrist and pulled her around. Beck pried the axe from her hand. "Get in the house, children. All of you, get in the house. What happened here, August?" He pushed Lottie toward the door. "Get in the house Lottie."

August ran up the steps. She yelled back over her shoulder. "That child took away an apple I gave Sheffield. He bit her. It was his apple. I gave it to him."

"Keep your crazy wife away from me. Them are my best apples. If someone had planted trees on your side of the house, then your children wouldn't have to steal to get them like the half breeds they are. If that woman so much as comes near me or my family again, I'll turn you in to the mill manager. They'll put you out. Do you hear me? There are rules to live by for these houses."

"Yeah, I hear you. The manager might be interested in the way you call people names and make trouble for your neighbors. That's in that rule book along with no fighting. It's six of one and half dozen of the other in rule breaking, don't you think? You leave my family alone. I could hear you screaming at them all the way to the bottom of the hill. What was one little apple going to hurt? August couldn't climb the tree, so it had to be on the ground. I'm sorry about the biting, but both of them are just babies. I'll take care of Sheffield. You talk to your child about taking something away from another."

"Keep that lunatic woman inside your house." She shook her fist at Lottie.

Beck stared hard at the woman. "I don't think that'll happen. For one thing, it's too hot. Another thing...If I was you, I'd try not to make her that upset again. She's from a family with a long history of feuds and revenge killings. That ain't no threat but, if I was you, I'd take it as a warning."

He couldn't help but laugh out loud at the look of fear on the woman's face. Not that he thought Lottie would ever act on her feelings, but anything was possible. Especially after the ruckus he had come home to today.

Inside the house, tears turned to sobs that shook Lottie's body. "She's a witch. You're supposed to burn a witch at the stake. She was hissing at us, all wild-eyed and pointing her bony finger at me. My children are no worse than hers. Hers are little snakes in the grass. The only difference is my children don't hide their bad deeds. Those little devils of hers try to look like angels to everyone. They ain't angels, unless they're the devil's angels. I saw one of the older ones in the store the other day pick up a piece of candy while the keeper wasn't looking. He put it right in his pocket. She saw him do it and never said a word."

Beck's chest heaved, and he blew out a long breath. "Take my word for it, you can't let the Hooper and Watson rise up in you. We're a long way from home for you to be starting a feud with people we barely know."

"Barely know? I don't even know their name. She knows all about me, or thinks she does, yet I don't know them. I don't like it here but, if we have to stay, I'll tend to my business if they'll tend to theirs."

Beck stared at Lottie. "That sounds like the right thing to do, but from what I have seen, this place has to become your family in order to survive it. Down at the mill, it's like they're one big family. They tease each other and seem to know everything there is to know about the ones they work with or live around. I asked someone about that. They said that since you are together more hours a day at the mill than you are at home, they are your family. Having ill will would make things hard on all of us."

Lottie said, 'I'm sick of hearing about your mill family. Annie May's mill family. They are NOT your family. We're your family." She swept her hands toward the children and then at herself.

"Lottie, please."

Lottie pointed her finger at Beck. "These people are heathens. I hate every last one of 'em."

"The people's name next door is Finley. Try to get to know them. It's easy to think a particular person is all good or all bad. But the truth of the matter, those two things weave in and out in any one person. They're two sides to the same coin, mixing and mingling inside a person. I've seen it in myself." He stopped and reached out to her. "I've seen that way in you. You shouldn't feel hatred toward your neighbor."

"Lordy, Beck, you can't tell me what my feelings ought to be. I can't even tell myself that. Those feelings just come up of their own accord as do my thoughts. Maybe I shouldn't act in a particular way, but feelings are a different story."

Beck raked his hand through his wet hair. *Lordy, what an end to the first week of living in a town! I sure hope it gets better and not worse.*

Chapter 6

December 1900

It was hard to believe that the quietest, most peaceful place Lottie had found in their four weeks in Clifton was in a cemetery on Vinegar Hill. This was the first graveyard where she didn't know a soul that was buried in it. The dream she had in Tennessee stayed on her mind and whispered every bad detail. She couldn't get it out of her mind. If it came true, it would be while the babies were still young, seeing that all three had been small caskets. They could very well end up here.

She knew she shouldn't hate everyone in Clifton, but she was mighty close to it. All the people appeared unfriendly and downright horrible. Last night, while in the bed and everyone asleep, Lottie had thought about Beck's claim of her being bad and good, according to what she was feeling. It might be true, but there were bad people in the world. Some were really bad. She had married one....Owen. As for the people in Clifton, her thoughts brought her to the conclusion that these people were pretty much like apples in a basket. There were good ones, and there were rotten ones. It would be necessary for her to learn early on how to separate the two in her mind. If she didn't, soon all of them would look rotten to her, much like they did today. She couldn't afford to be soured on life at her age.

She walked among the graves and read dates and names. These people had about the nicest tomb rocks she'd ever seen. She stopped and read from a small tombstone with a rose carved in the stone. *A little bud of love, to bloom with God above.* The death date was July of this year, 1900. Lottie put her fist to her mouth and bit on her fingers.

Further down was a grave surrounded by a cast iron picket fence with twirled flowers along the edges. It bordered all four sides of the grave. It was about two feet high in a scalloped pattern and more roses where each metal piece met. She stepped to the end and read from the stone. "Clara, daughter of A and H Cobb, born Nov 18, 1896, died Jan 13, 1898"

She put a hand on each side of her face. "Poor baby girl. Never got to see what life was about."

A voice behind her spoke softly. "Then again, she never will know the troubles of life. She's in a better place." The woman came and stood beside her.

Lottie bit her lip, and there were tears in her eyes.

"Was she yours?" Lottie asked and watched the woman's face.

"No. She was my sister's baby." She took the hand full of fall mums she clutched, leaned over, and laid them at the base of the tombstone. "My sister and her husband moved away a few months after Clara died. I promised her I'd see that flowers were sometimes put on her grave, at least as long as I live here." She walked to the tree beside the grave and leaned against it. "I guess I'll be here all my life. Nothing seems to bother my husband enough to leave. Not even babies that die right and left at least two times a year. He thinks he's lucky enough for it to not happen to us. I'm not so sure. Death seems to have no respect of person or age. It don't care who you are…how good or bad your family is, either. It comes most of the time in the dark of the night like it did with Moses in the Bible when the first born children were taken from Pharaoh's people."

Lottie glanced around the graveyard. "There's a right smart of baby graves. That's for sure. Where I come from, we'd have an epidemic come through about every two or three years, but not as often as here. Two a year, you say? It can't be healthy, everybody living this close to each other."

"You're from the mountains, I hear."

Lottie raised her eyebrows.

"It's a growing town, but not much happens here that escapes being gossiped about. Your neighbor told everybody you were an Indian and threatened to scalp her."

"She wasn't far from wrong. In the scalping, I mean." Lottie laughed and her face was red as a beet. "She called me and my children names. It was tempting to claw her eyes out, but I mostly wanted to scare her enough to leave us alone." She reached her hand out to the woman. "I'm Lottie Radford. My husband is Beck. I was a Watson before I married."

"I'm Florence Teague. My husband is Lafayette but we all call him Fate. Good to meet you, Lottie. I can see we could be good friends. I like you a lot. You have enough pluck to actually make it in this God-forsaken town. You have to give as much as you get, or some of these people will make your life miserable."

Florence sat down on a large rock. Lottie sat down on the ground.

"I suppose that's what I was doing then with that mean ole woman that lives next to me. If Beck...that's my husband...hadn't stopped me, I'd be carrying her scalp on my belt now." Lottie ran her finger through the strip of material she used as a belt.

Florence laughed. "You said you're not an Indian."

"No, I'm not, but she called my children half-breeds, so I decided to show her how Indians act." Lottie patted her side. "That scalp would be right here, to show everyone you cannot mess with a

Hooper or a Watson." She wrinkled her nose and smiled at Florence.

"Oh Lottie, you're the funniest person I ever met. What would you have done if Beck hadn't stopped you?"

Lottie smiled. "I'm not sure. I could've gone through with it. The Hooper side of my family likes to fight. She made me that mad. She's a witch."

Florence chuckled. "Then burn her at the stake, but don't scalp her." She sat up straight and pulled her dress tail down over her feet. "There are some mean people in this world, that's for sure. But there's a little good in everyone. At least I tell myself that.

"You sound like my Beck now. Those were almost his very words."

There were sticks lying on her niece's grave inside the fence, and Florence reached through and picked them off. She laid them in her apron and stood up. "I have to get home. I live two houses down from you."

They walked together until a tree was in their path. Florence went to the left and Lottie started to the right. Lottie stopped, and came back and followed Florence to the left.

Florence was curious. "Why did you do that?"

Lottie turned red. "My mama always told me, 'never let a tree split the path of you and a friend or you'll soon quarrel'. I certainly don't want to have a fuss with the only friend I've made so far."

Florence bent over in laughter. Lottie bit her lip and gave a small smile.

"Yes, that's for sure. I like you a lot. I don't believe we'll ever quarrel. Come and see me soon." Florence waved good bye.

Lottie smiled. "I'll do that. You come up to my house anytime, too. I'd be glad for the company." She stood and watched her new friend walk out of the graveyard and onto the road. Out of the corner of her eye, there was a flash of a black buggy that passed to her right with two men inside. It passed Florence, but she never looked up. It disappeared into the air before the road turned. There was no dust or sound."

Lottie reached out and pushed her hand against the tree where Florence had stood just minutes before. She felt weak and closed her eyes for a moment. When she opened them, the woman was out of sight.

"No." She choked on the word. "Why do things like this happen to me? I don't want to know what this means. Don't show me. We're not even close acquaintances, yet. If there's nothing I can do, why show me?" Lottie looked up into the sky and waved her arm. "Why me? Why her? Why now?" She put her hand on her heart. "I hoped that when I left Jackson County this foolishness would all be behind me. Instead, I'm seeing more and more things to come. This is such a burden to bear."

Chapter 7

December 1900

Lottie put a pot of beans on the stove to start to boil while she cooked breakfast, as she did most days. She sent the others to work and let the fire die. The heat from the stove would be enough to finish cooking the beans for supper. Cold weather had come, and Lottie enjoyed cooking when the house felt warm with the heat from the cooking stove.

Lottie heard Misses Findley yell at her baby to quit crying. Almost everything the woman said appeared to be yelled. Lottie threw dishwater from the back door. She stood outside and looked at the house two doors down. That was where Florence lived.

Behind Florence's house was a small fire burning under an iron pot. A washboard lay on the ground nearby. In a moment, she came out the back door with an arm full of clothes that she dropped into the steaming water. Lottie watched her scrape a piece of lye soap and let the shavings fall into the water. She picked up a mallet and pushed and tugged at the clothes.

Florence looked toward Lottie, smiled, and waved.

Lottie grabbed a coat and ran to the back of the other woman's house. "Hello Florence. I'm glad you came outside. I've wanted to stop by since we met. This was my first chance."

"Glad you did. Sorry I'm so busy, but that's the good thing about talk. You can do it and work. Well, at least some people can." Florence turned her head with her ear aimed at Lottie's house. "I can hear your neighbor scream all the way down here. I can only image how loud she is when you're under the same roof."

Lottie looked toward the house. "I hear them talking in there. At least he talks. She yells. I never knew there were houses where two families that don't even know each other could live together."

Florence laughed. "Well, pretty much every house here is like that. There are a few that are not…the ones where the bosses live are one family houses. Your house neighbors are Oliver and Novella Finley."

"Who's your house neighbor?" Lottie looked at the house that was identical to hers.

"Their name is Smith." She looked at Lottie and raised her eyebrows. "At least that's what they say."

Lottie's eyes grew large, and Florence laughed. "I'm just teasing you. I've known them all my life. The wife grew up beside me in Spartanburg. They moved here to Hurricane Shoals...well, it's called Clifton now, of course...when they went to work at the mill. It seems easy to joke with you. I know it's all strange to someone that's always lived in the mountains."

The wooden mallet Florence picked up made a perfect tool to push the clothes around in the water. She swished it back and forth. Lottie would ask Beck if he could make her one. Normally she let the water cool, and she rubbed each piece of clothing against the rough rub-board her papa had made when she married. Someday she wanted to get a store-bought one.

"Florence, why don't you work at the Mill?" Lottie asked.

"It's because of my Papa. When I married Fate, Papa made him promise he wouldn't make me work in the mill. Papa was lying on his death bed at the time. We're not sure what the sickness was, but Papa swore it was from working in the mill day in and day out. All that dust he had to breathe. It got to where he coughed from the minute he got to work until he went home. Then it was all the time, even at the house. He didn't want me in that mill at all!"

"I don't mind working if it would help our family get ahead. We seem to be hand to mouth with our money. Beck wants a farm, and I want to go back to the mountains to be near Papa and Mama."

Florence smiled. "I'm glad you don't work there. Your family may not get sick, but I hated watching my daddy lose his breath and run out in the yard to try to get it back. He'd breathe so hard, the air sounded wheezy coming out. The sickness started about a year after he left the farm and started to work in the mill. He worked there two more years until it was too hard to catch his breath. In another two years he had passed. Before he passed away, he made Fate promise I wouldn't have to work there. We were only courting then, but Papa knew we'd marry."

Lottie wrinkled her forehead. "Will my Beck get sick?"

"No one knows who will and who won't. Not everybody does. Fate has worked there four years, and he's just fine and dandy."

Florence wrung out the clothes after rinsing in the clear cold water of another tub. Lottie took them to the yard and laid them across the wire that was strung between two poles.

"You don't have to do that." Florence took a shirt by the shoulders and whipped it in the air. Most all the wrinkles fell out.

Lottie laughed. "I know, but I want to talk longer, so I should at least have the decency to help you work."

"What else do you want to talk about?"

"Beck has my children working in the mill, too. I don't like it, but it seems most children here are working. They should be in school. I took my children by the schoolhouse and met the teacher. She's nice, but it seemed like she was in a tizzy trying to sort out who to send to work today and who to let stay in the classroom. My children can read and write, but I want them to learn all they can."

Florence put another load of clothes into the same hot water and stirred with the mallet.

"There are lots of children working. When I have children, I'll be like you. I hope they don't work in a mill. There are lots of injuries to men, women, and children. Those are the perils of public work, I reckon."

"I suppose I've malingered long enough." Lottie laughed. "That's a new word for me. Beck taught it to me. They were warned against him or the children 'malingering'. I never thought I'd get a chance to use such an expression."

"Fate wanted me to ask if your husband plays a musical instrument. My man can play about anything that has a string on it."

"Beck doesn't play, but my Papa was like your man. I sure miss good music."

"Y'all come over any time you want on a Saturday night or Sunday. We have a good time right on the front porch, at least till the neighbors run everybody off. They only do that if it's really late. In the summer, Fate plays with a bunch of people down on the sand bar by the dam. That's where we go to have a good time."

Lottie waved and headed back to start her own wash.

Chapter 8

May 1901

Lottie shook out spilled flour from the hand-hooked rug. She stood on the edge of the porch and jerked it back and forth. A glimmer of red in the east flushed the dark sky. She listened to the low voices in the rooms where the Findley's lived. A baby cried, and she heard the mother shush it. Before the sun could spill enough light to make their way to Dexter Mill, her husband, Beck, and two of her children would come out of the house and run to beat the shrill whistle that marked the change to the day shift.

It was hard to believe they'd been in Clifton for seven months. Spring had been early and there had already been several hot days.

She turned toward the creaking sound of a wagon. She looked up and saw a horse-drawn hearse. An oil rag torch was on either side of the driver to light the way. She leaned against the post and put her hand over her heart. As long as she lived, she'd never forget the feeling she had each time she saw one in the darkness of early morning of the Clifton hillside. She stood and watched it pass, then shook the rug again.

Down the road, a woman screamed. "No. No. No. Let me have my baby. She's not dead. I saw her take a breath just before you came. Who sent for you?" Lottie saw the faint outline of the hearse had pulled up to the house several doors down. She noticed from the light of the torches, two men stood at the door of the house.

She sat down on the steps and looked up at the mill house where she lived. It was smack dab like the one in her dream seven months ago. Her heart felt heavy with dread. She'd seen a hearse just like the one down the road...three trips to her house, each time leaving with a small casket. Lottie cried.

They called her the *sighted* sister. In spite of what her Mama said, knowing something was going to happen before it did was a curse and not a gift. In her letters to Sugar, she said that she prayed every day that the dreams and visions would go away. Why did she have to be the one that was born with the veil over her face? Why didn't God give the gift to one of her brothers or sisters?

Lottie listened to the hacking cough that came from inside of her own house. Two and half year old Sheffield was in the house burning up with fever. Money for medicine was hard to come by. It took all that Beck, twelve-year-old son Brody, and eleven-year-old Annie May, could make working in the mill to pay for the house they lived in and buy food.

Beck came out of the house, followed by Brody and Annie May. "We're going to the mill. We'll be home at the usual time."

Lottie stood up. "Annie May, where's your dinner bucket?"

Annie May jumped off the porch, acted like she didn't hear, and ran to meet a friend coming down the road.

"She best not be forgetting the one thing that'll give her strength enough to work in that hot mill. There's not enough for y'all to share in either one of your buckets. She'll be hungry by supper time."

Brody waved at a boy that stood in the street in front of their house. "There's Elliott. I'm going to walk with him to the mill."

Lottie peeked inside the door. "I hear Sheffield talking in his sleep. His fever must be getting higher. I can't get him to eat a bite. He has the shaking chills ever so often, too. His skin is blue and he's working hard at breathing. I'm a-feared its influenza. I need to get some kind of remedy. I wish we lived near Mama. She'd know what to give him, something from the woods."

Beck pushed his hat onto his head. "Don't mention influenza unless you're sure. If they suspect that, you'll be sent to Pest Row."

"What's Pest Row?" Lottie wrinkled her forehead.

"It's up the hill from the bridge, left on Valley Street, a slight left on Cedar Street, and then turn a sharp right. There are two long buildings where they put anyone that has something catching. It has eight rooms and a kitchen for everyone to share. You'd have to go with him. There's no one else to take care of them. You're needed here. There's been so many die that they have to do something to keep everyone from getting the sickness. So far, Pest Row has only been used for small pox, but you and me both know that influenza kills. Just don't get him outside or let him near anybody until we know. I'll be able to get some turpentine and camphor for the fever after we get paid tomorrow. Everybody says that's the best you can give for a fever. I'll see if the company store will let me charge our food until next pay day."

Lottie nodded and went into the house.

***

Brody ran to the spring on the upper side of the Mill. This was where most of the women and girls ate their lunch. He hopped on one foot and the other and turned bright red. "Annie May, here's my dinner bucket. You forgot your food. I'm not going to eat mine today so you can have it. Elliott and I got ahead on our doffing. The bobbins are full and ready for the frame and a few to spare. We're ahead of the girls that are spinning, that way we can go down to the river and swim after everyone comes back from eating. We won't be gone but a little bit. We'll never be missed."

Annie May took the food and looked at Brody. "You best not be caught down by the river. You know the foreman watches every minute to make sure we all work. No malingering, he said. Papa will be mad if you get caught doing anything that could make you lose your job."

"I'll be careful. Elliott has done it lots of times, he says. We did it twice last week. We put in our fair time of working, but we do it different than the others."

Elliott ran up to them and slapped Brody on the back. "Come on. We've got to hurry."

They ran down the bank and hid between the rocks until a group of men passed on their way up to the mill from where they had eaten dinner down by the river.

Brody reached up and jerked his shirt over his head. One swift pull and off went his breeches. He threw them to the side and dove into the cold water.

Elliott looked at the cotton mill. "We've got to get back to work. I saw the boss standing by the window. I'm not sure there's time for the swim. He'll have our hide if we don't get back in there. You talked too long to Annie May."

Brody treaded water. "I only said a word or two to her. Come on. We'll swim a bit and then get our clothes back on and hightail it inside. We've earned a few minutes being we worked whilst the others were eating. The boss will be watching the others as they start to work.""

Elliott was convinced and took his clothes off down to his bare body. He dove in and swam toward the middle of the river.

"Get back over this way. They'll see us." Brody heard a door slam and swam closer to the rocks. When he could touch bottom, he hid from the angry man tearing down the river bank toward them.

"You scoundrel, Elliott Treadway. You're a lazy, good for nothing boy, no better than your father. Get yourself up here right now. Get your clothes on. You're coming with me.

Elliott looked at the foreman, and then glanced at where he saw Brody go to hide. He could see neither hide nor hair of him.

Before Elliott got his shirt buttoned, the foreman drug him up the bank toward a group of men that watched the commotion.

"Treadway? Get out here, Jonathan Treadway."

Elliott's dad came to where the foreman stood, holding his son by the neck of his shirt.

"Get a leather strap someone." A man ran into the mill and came back with a strap.

"Treadway, your son was swimming instead of working. I want you to take this strap and beat him right now. He needs the laziness beat out of him. That'll make him think twice about being a slacker on the job."

Jonathan's face flushed. "I'm not laying a hand on him. He's just a boy. He worked through dinner and took a few minutes to rest. He don't deserve no beating for that. Besides, you done beat the devil out of him too many times since we worked here."

The foreman came and stood in front of Jonathan. "Back on the farm, you may have worked on your own time, but here you work on mine! You beat him, or you're both fired. There's a group of men that would love to take your job in a minute, if they're asked. Do what I say and do it now. Take the whip and beat him."

The two men stood eye to eye without a blink. Jonathan reached behind him and grabbed his son's hand. "Come on Elliott. It's time we move on."

"Papa!"

"Come on I said. You don't deserve no beating for what any boy would've done. Even this here foreman's boy would've wanted to swim on a pretty day like this."

"You're fired, the boy for mischief and you for not keeping your son under control. Get out of here...you and the boy."

Brody ran up the hill and stood in front of the foreman. His clothes were dripping wet.

"Wait. You can't fire him. He's been working hard all day. We both have. As hard as anyone in that mill. We didn't do no harm. Everything is caught up for the other workers. We did our job."

The foreman reached out and grabbed Brody by the shoulder. "So you've been swimming on company time too, have you? Beck Radford, get over here right now."

Beck came and looked from the wet Brody to the foreman.

"You take this here strap and beat that son of yours until you're sure he'll never do this again. If you don't, you'll be fired just like the Treadways."

Jonathan and Elliott backed up but did not leave.

Brody wiped his eyes. "It ain't fair. We didn't do nothing wrong. We both worked while everybody else ate. We wasn't going to take but a dip. It was less time than you took to eat your dinner, Mr. Foreman. Elliott and his Papa shouldn't be fired."

The foreman ignored Brody's pleas and looked back at Beck. "Take the strap to him, or you're out of here."

Beck swallowed hard. "Let me talk to the boy first. Then I'll do what you ask."

He pulled Brody to the side and bent his head close to his son's ear. "I know as well as you that you don't deserve no whupping. But I can't do what Jonathan just did for his son. I can't stand up for you this time. I need this job and I need it bad. We all have to eat. Your Mama is in the family way, and it's soon to be born, and your younger brother is sick and needs medicine. If I don't work, I can't get that for him, and I can't feed the rest of you. Work is hard to come by, especially if word gets around to the other mills about what has happened here."

Brody scrunched his face, and tears came up in his eyes.

"I need you to take this like a man. I'll beat you like he says, but you know that I think it's wrong.

We'll have to do what we have to do to keep our jobs. Do you hear me? Don't give him the satisfaction of hearing you cry. You swallow those tears, and don't you make a sound."

Brody nodded and began to shake like a leaf in the wind. Chill bumps raised up over his body as the wind blew over him.

They walked back together, and Beck took the strap and raised it over his head. It came down with a pop as it hit Brody's back. Three more times, he hit him. Whelps rose up on this back. A stream of blood ran down his chin from the cut on his lip where he had bit it so hard to keep from yelling.

Beck threw the strap at the foot of the foreman. He grabbed Brody's shirt from off the ground and helped him put it on.

"That ain't good enough. You need to beat him more. You didn't even make him cry."

Beck jerked around and stared at the foreman. He narrowed his eyes and gritted his teeth. "I hit him plenty hard enough. He has whelps on his back from the leather. I ain't hitting him again with that strap. I did what you said, and now I'm going back to work." He turned back to Brody. "Get back to doffing! Lines are stopped waiting on you."

The foreman stared at their backs. He looked around to the others. "All of you get back to work. This ain't no ballgame. It's past work time." He looked at Jonathan and Elliott. "You two get off the grounds. Get your family, and get out of the company's house. I don't want to see you anywhere around here again."

***

Beck came in the house, went to the table, and sat down. Lottie reached over Beck's shoulder and set down a pan of bread. She stepped back.

Brody slammed the door, pushed between Beck and Lottie, and ran into his room and closed the door.

Lottie yelled. "Get back in here Brody, and eat your supper. You can't work as hard as you do and not eat. You'll get weak."

Brody came back and sat down beside Annie May. He kept his head bent low over his chest.

Lottie wiped her hands on her apron and looked at Beck's grim face and the top of Brody's head. "What's wrong with you two?"

Beck stared straight into Lottie's eyes. "Nothing's wrong. Just put the rest of supper on the table and let's eat."

Lottie glanced at Annie May. "Do you know what's wrong?"

Annie May shook her head no and grabbed a fork.

Lottie sat down on the end of the bench and faced Beck. "I know good and well something's wrong. Now, what is it?"

Brody raised his head slightly and looked at Beck's face.

"It's all done and past. There's nothing to talk about. We have food on the table, and we're going to thank the good Lord for it and eat." Beck looked to each one then bowed his head.

"Thank you, Lord, for this here food. Thank you that we still have jobs and can put food in our bellies. Thank you for making us strong enough to do what we have to do. Amen."

Lottie watched a tear slide down Brody's face and drip onto his pants. She wanted to grab him and kiss his sad face like she had when he was a baby. But something made him look grown up today…a man. He wouldn't take kindly to hugs from his Mama.

She grabbed a plate and put some potatoes on it. She mashed them with a fork and added some potato water until it was soupy. "I'm going to try to get some of this down Sheffield. He's so weak he can barely hold up his head."

Beck looked over at the child lying on a pallet between their bed and the door. He was still and his face red with fever. "I'll get paid tomorrow. I'll go by the doctor and see if I can buy medicine. I wish I could've gotten it earlier this week, but we didn't have the money. There are probably fifty children that work at Mill Two down with the fever. We're short-handed every day. They told us today that ten have died over at Mill Three."

Lottie cried softly as she slipped the spoon between Sheffield's parched lips. Annie May got up from the table and got two cloths. She went to the back porch and wet them. One she laid on Sheffield's head and, with the other, she pulled up the back of his shirt and washed his hot body.

Beck and Brody stared at each other. Beck nodded, and Brody sat up straight in his chair and shook his head. They both knew that they had done what had to be done to get that medicine. Now if Sheffield would get better, it would be worth the pain.

Chapter 9

May 1901

The sun glowed bright red over the western sky. It was a sure sign of stormy weather before the day was through. Lottie held Sheffield in her arms. She pulled the blanket tighter around the shivering body. Glazed eyes looked up at her and filled with tears. She sat him up, and started to stand up and take him into the house. Before she rose to her feet, there was slight wind that blew from the northwest. She looked to her right. Floating toward her was dark material like a sheet. It fluttered in the wind, but never lowered far enough that she could see the top of it.

Lottie felt sick when the sheeting material floated near the porch roof and stayed there. Her breath caught in her throat. She looked back down at Sheffield. When she looked up, the sheet rose up and slowly floated up the hill. Lottie stood and tightened her arms around her son. The sheet stopped and hung over the cemetery. She moved to the edge of the porch to see where it would go.

"No. Oh no! Don't go down. Please don't go down." It swooped down into the cemetery and disappeared.

Lottie threw back her head and moaned. "Oh God....my God. Nooooooo. Please stop it. Stop these visions. This is not a gift. It's a curse. Why can't you let this sickness leave?" Lottie sat back down in the rocking chair.

Beck came through the door pulling at his breeches. "What's wrong with you?"

Lottie's face was pale, and she began to tremble. She pulled tightly on the limp body in her arms. "It's another sign like I had before. This thing is trying to take my family from me, one baby at a time." The child inside of her rolled to the side and stretched. She grabbed her belly with one hand. Its feet pushed against her ribs, and she threw her upper body backward.

"What was the sign?" Beck looked at Lottie's face.

She didn't want to, but she had to tell him the dream she had in Tennessee. She cried as she told him each detail. It was as clear in her mind as if she had dreamt the night before.

Beck reached and tried to take Sheffield from her arms.

Lottie screamed at him. "Don't you worry yourself about the dream. Leave Sheffield be. He's going to be fine. I'll not let this sickness take him. I swear I won't."

Beck went to the jar hidden in the flour barrel and emptied the money into his hand. "I'm going to get the doctor. I know we promised to play like we didn't have this money, but we need a doctor now. We can't wait for pay day."

Lottie cried and pulled Sheffield into her arms and rocked.

***

A half hour later, Sheffield's eyes opened slightly and he fixed his eyes on his Mama. Lottie was afraid to blink. She wanted him to see her looking at him every second that they had left.

Shortly before Beck and the doctor returned, a gurgle slipped through his small, dry lips. There was a rattle in his chest with each breath.

Lottie stood up with Sheffield in her arms, then turned around and stilled the rocker. Her mama told her to leave a rocking chair moving would bring on death.

She turned as Beck came up the steps. "Send the doctor on his way. We won't need him here, but there probably will be lots of others that will need him very soon. It's too late for us. There's nothing any of us can do."

***

They sat on the front seat of the church. Beck was on the end, then her, Brody, Annie May, and August. She pulled her dress loosely over her swollen belly.

She had attended church irregularly as of lately. Not because of lack of desire to be there but because there was too much to do. She had taken Sheffield to church a week and a half ago, along with the other children, out of guilt, even though he had coughed the entire service. Beck hadn't attended church in quite a while. He had when they first came, but he had stopped and would not tell her the reason. Today he looked uncomfortable. He never tried to stop her when there came a time that she could go. You could tell by the people's less than friendly handshakes, that they felt them to be the worst kind of sinners.

Lottie didn't speak to anyone. One by one, they came by and learned forward slightly. Not near enough to touch her but where she could hear them when they quietly whispered how sorry they were. She stared straight ahead and nodded. Beck had told her that the preacher said no one would come unless the casket was nailed shut. They knew he died of the fever. There was fear in their face, and mothers kept their small children behind them and covered by their skirts. Lottie heard it in the way they murmured when they gathered far enough away that she could not understand their words. She knew how they felt. She wished she hadn't gone any place for the past month and taken her children. If only her family didn't work in that disease-infested mill. Any one of the family could have brought the fever home to Sheffield. There was so much sickness in most all the mill houses. We could have gotten the illness here at church. Today, a teenage girl sat on the seat near them and coughed every other breath the whole service. The people behind her got up and left. The ones beside her moved to the other side of the church. She wished she could leave, too.

Lottie's eyes rolled back in her head and she moaned softly. *Why could it not be me laying there?*

The preacher went to the pulpit. He held both sides of the sacred desk and looked at Lottie and Beck. He spoke directly at them.

It didn't take long to see that he was blaming them for the death of their son. He preached that when people don't come to the house of God, there's a curse that comes down. He talked about the sins of the world and people leaving their vows and marrying another while their first companion still lived. It was the strangest message for a funeral she had ever heard.

Beck looked at Lottie and raised his eyebrows. She scrooched up her shoulders to her neck and let them fall. She had no idea how the preacher knew about their first marriages. She looked down the row of children to her side and saw August's face turn red. Lottie took a deep breath and closed her eyes. No doubt August had told someone, and they had told somebody else. Of course, no one offered to ask why she was not with her first husband. No one cared that Owen killed their baby and had almost killed her more than once. They were labeled as bad sinners sitting in a church house with a dead baby, and it was entirely their own fault. Lottie wondered what he said to the ones that lost babies that were married to their first husband or wife. *Who's he going to blame in that event?* Lottie stopped listening to him.

It was a good thing that the preacher stopped speaking and everyone rose to their feet for prayer. Otherwise, he and the others could have watched her hastily take her children out the side door of the church.

Beck picked up the tiny box he had fashioned, and Lottie had laid Sheffield in that morning. He walked to her side and set the casket on the ground. He reached out and grabbed Lottie, but she jerked away.

"I'm sorry I let him die, Lottie."

Lottie turned and looked at him. "Twasn't your fault. How could you have stopped it? It was meant to be, I guess. Maybe it was my doing. I was the one that saw this happen whilst we were still in Tennessee. Maybe I shouldn't have come here. It might have been best if I had left you and went back home. Or maybe it was the fact that I saw all this was going to happen that actually *made* it happen. It would be my fault then. I don't blame you."

"Don't say that, Lottie. It ain't your fault. I brought you to this town in hopes of a better life. It's because of me. "You can't help what things you see with the gift. I heard tell about people like you before, but I'd never met one."

Lottie's face screwed up, and she began to shake. "A person like me? A gift? They say it's a gift. Why do they keep calling it that? It ain't, you know. Nobody in their right mind would call this a gift."

People gathered behind them, but stayed back away from the grave. Beck turned his head and studied their faces. Nobody spoke a word. He carried the box with one hand, and grabbed Lottie's arm and guided her to the hole in the ground he and a friend had dug earlier.

***

Lottie refused to listen to the comforting words that the preacher decided to say at the grave side. He had delivered his real message to them in the church. The old 'dust to dust, and ashes to ashes' he added, and the hope he spoke of meeting this innocent baby when we all get to heaven, made vomit come up in her throat. She planned on meeting Sheffield in paradise. She just didn't need the preacher to judge her before she got before God. She figured God knew the whole story and would be a little better able to judge fairly.

At the edge of the cemetery, Florence sat down on a root beside the tree where Lottie had squatted.

They both watched the men throw dirt on top of Sheffield's wooden box.

"I don't know what to say, Lottie. This has to be more than a woman can bear. I ain't never lost a child to death. I had a brother and sister to die of the fever when I was a child, but I don't think that is anything I can judge this by. Your own flesh and blood dying in your arms has to tear your heart right out. I know my sister fainted when Clara died. She didn't speak for days. She wasn't worth a cent for the funeral."

Lottie wrapped her hands around her upper arms. "Death is something that a person doesn't ever get used to. For some people, sorrow comes suddenly, like it did when your sister lost her daughter. But it comes slowly for me, and it lingers a long time. People say that grief washes over them the minute a death happens. But I sit and think about the baby that has died, and I start to realize we won't ever laugh together. I'll never get to say I love you to them again and watch their eyes get all dancey and bright. Those same words will never be heard by me from their mouth. Some would say it's easier if it comes slow, but I differ. It's a hard burden to stretch out the pain, but I can't seem to help myself. Laughter is hard to come by for months and months afterwards." She looked down and grabbed Florence's hand that lay by her side. "A child's death puts fear in your heart every time you wake in the middle of the night and don't hear any sounds coming from the other children. Then you worry about the crying, AND you worry about the quiet. Dawn comes as a relief. There's no way to ever hide from what you know...that death seems final. The preacher talks to you about how you'll meet again, but that makes you ponder all the time that will pass, and if they'll even know who you are."

Florence choked back a sob. "Oh, Lottie, that's too sad to think about."

Lottie looked around the graveyard. "Do you think there'll ever be a time when at least half of the children a woman bears will be able to make it to become grown? When sickness no longer yanks the babies from our arms time after time? My Mama says it's been this way since time began. If they can make trains and automobiles, it seems to me that surely they can make a body where, when it gets sick, would be able to get well with good medicine. I want my babies to get to see a full life."

Florence squeezed her friend's hand and looked out at all the short graves that were marked with rocks at head and foot. "I hope they find a way to stop these fevers. If not, there ain't going to be enough space in this cemetery for the graves."

Lottie laid her head on Florence's shoulder. "This town should be called Sorrow. It seems we all live in an unending state of mourning. Everybody has some member of the family or a close friend that the sickness has taken from them. I propose they change the name of Clifton to Sorrow, South Carolina. The rain would be our tears wetting the earth. We breathe the air of heartache. The fog is nothing but our misery as it leaves our bodies. Gloom makes the shadows at night. All our nights are starless, and our days reveal the clouds that refuse to let the sun shine through." Lottie's tears dripped from her jaw. "I want to move far from here. Forget all that has happened in my life. I want to wake up and be a new person with no memories to haunt me."

They had either kept Sheffield inside long enough, or maybe it was not influenza, but very few others died that month. Lottie was thankful. There were no new graves for a while.

***

Two weeks later, as Beck pushed a bolt of material into the Cloth Room, the foreman came over and spoke close to his ear. "You are needed down at the company store."

"What for?"

"I think your wife is in need of help. Hurry back." The foreman motioned for a man to take Beck's place.

"What is wrong?"

Why would she be at the company store? She don't have money to spend down there.

Lottie had stacked the dishes and placed them in a wash pan just before he left that morning. Nothing had seemed wrong.

The foreman raised his eyebrows. "I guess you'll have to go and see. They said to tell you to hurry."

***

Lottie was sitting on the front steps in her gown when Beck got to the store. A sheet lay at her feet. The storekeeper and his wife stood behind her. Three women were by the front door whispering.

The storekeeper came to his side. "You need to take your wife home Beck. She came down here in her gown tail. My wife tried to cover her up, but she threw the sheet on the ground. I asked her what she wanted. She just stared at me like she didn't know who I was or even who she was. I can see she has no idea where she is."

"Lottie, get up and let's go home. You'll catch your death of cold in this weather." Beck pulled on her arm.

Lottie smiled. "My Mama doesn't let me go with the likes of you." She pulled her arm away from him. "You're too handsome for your own good." She laughed out loud. Too loud.

Beck turned in a circle and looked at those that had gathered to watch Lottie. They stopped talking and watched him.

"Go home people. Give her some room. She just buried her baby two weeks ago. She needs rest, that's all."

Beck pulled Lottie to her feet and put his arm around her. She giggled like a school girl. "Don't you know all these people will talk behind our back if you act so friendly with me?"

"They're just jealous if they do." He whispered in her ear and she laughed. She went with him to their house.

August sat on the steps, and lined up acorn tops in a row across the porch.

"Did you see your Mama leave?"

August looked at her mother. Lottie was pale and stared like she did not know her own daughter.

"I did see her leave. I tried to go with her, but she made me stay here. She called me Sugar and said she didn't need a chaperone today as all the men were working. I didn't know what she meant, but I stayed here like she said. This morning, she had a squally time after you went to work, but she seemed happy again when she left the house."

Together, Beck and August led Lottie to bed.

"You stay close to your Mama until I get home from work. Don't let her go traipsing over the neighborhood. Find a way to get her to stay here if she tries to leave."

"Papa, I can't make Mama stay here if she don't want to."

Lottie opened her eyes and stared at Beck. "I'm ok now. I keep hearing Sheffield cry, but when I go to the cries, he's nowhere to be found. A trip is what I need...just to get away from the house. I don't know what's wrong with me. I won't make you come home from work again, if I can help it." Tears filled her eyes. "Forgive me. I think I may have done things that would bring shame to you and the children. I can't seem to remember what I did, though."

"You didn't do anything to cause disgrace. No need for you to worry. It's all over and done with now."

She grabbed his left hand. "Sheffield won't cry anymore, will he?"

Beck covered his mouth with his right hand. He pulled his hand from hers and walked away.

***

When Beck and the children came home from work, supper was ready. August carried a stack of plates to the table. Lottie pushed a plate of cornbread into his hands. "Take this to the table, please."

"Are you all right?"

Lottie looked at him and raised her eyebrows. "Of course I'm all right. Why would you ask such a thing? You act like I've been sick. But, come to think of it, my throat has been sore this afternoon."

"You must've caught a chill while you were out visiting today."

"I ain't been out today. There was too much work to do here today to take a stroll. This house was a mess. I've cleaned all day long."

Chapter 10

June 1901

Beck was in the bedroom taking a washcloth bath. The girls laughed and chattered as they changed from work clothes into a nightgown.

"You girls need to hurry and get into bed. It's hard enough to get you up in the morning."

Annie May moaned. "It ain't even good and dark outside. I can't get to sleep until there's no light shining in the window."

Lottie saw a movement pass the edge of the bedroom window and stop near the window frame. It stayed there. She reached over and put her hands in the space where she saw a shadow. Lottie pulled back the edge of the skirt that she used for the curtain. At the sight outside, she pulled the whole thing down in one jerk and screamed.

"Lordy, there's a man peeping in the window. I'll teach him a thing or two." She ran through the kitchen and grabbed the iron skillet she had already placed on the stove for cooking the next morning. By the time she got outside, the man was running up the road in front of their house.

"You good for nothing, peeper. I'll beat your brains out with this skillet. You were looking inside on little girls as they change clothes. You've messed with the wrong woman this time. My family has killed for a whole lot less than this, you reprobate."

The girls looked out the door as their mama ran after him. The man turned into the woods at the end of the road and ran up toward Vinegar Hill.

Beck rushed to the front door and looked out over their head. "What's going on?"

Annie May laughed. "Some man was peeking in our window while we changed clothes. Mama took after him with a frying pan in her hand."

Beck sat down in a chair. "We're going to be the talk of the town, what with your Mama screaming all over this hillside. She is raving like a lunatic and telling her dreams and visions."

Lottie came back inside and set the skillet on the table by the door. She heard Beck talking about her. "What do you suppose I should do? Let him keep looking in at our daughter's naked bodies? You rather me pretend I didn't see him? Act like it never happened?"

Beck curled his lips in a snarl. He filled his jaws with air and stared at Lottie.

"If you were half a man, you'd be out there running him down for me."

"That's enough, Lottie. He didn't have no right doing what he did. I think he probably won't try that again after you threatened to beat his brains out. In fact, I doubt if anyone in this town would cross you now, what with this happening and the matter with the next door neighbor."

"Well good! That's all I want...for us to be left alone and live in peace." Lottie brushed her hands together.

Beck reached down and took off his shoes. He used the wet rag he had brought with him and washed his feet. "Surely you'd like to have at least one friend in Clifton. That's becoming highly unlikely."

"I have you to know I already have a friend. Her name is Florence, and she'd help me track this man down and take care of his wish to peek in windows. Maybe we could put his eyes out or remove something more important to him."

Beck ignored her plans. "So you made a friend. When did you do that?"

"Up in Vinegar Hill Cemetery. She was there to bring flowers to put on her niece's grave. We hit it off real good the first thing."

"Does she know about your history of feuds?"

Lottie stuck out her tongue at Beck. "She informed me that everyone in Clifton knows about the run-in I had with the neighbor."

Beck groaned. "I figured as much, though no one has said a word about it to me."

"I guess you don't have any friends close enough to tell you stories like that. I do."

The girls sat down and listened to them argue. Lottie turned and shooed them to bed.

"I may have to live here, but I don't have to like everyone that makes their home in Clifton. My friends are chosen by me and me alone. I never have cared much for what people thought about me. You must. If they treat me right, I'll treat them right. That's the end of the story. I ain't trying to make your life hard, but nobody is going to get by with peeping in on my girls or calling my family names. I plan on protecting them until my dying day."

***

Beck sat on the back step until everyone was quiet inside. He thought about the family that he was now a part of. It was unlike his other family or any other he knew. Lottie was braver and fiercer than he ever knew a woman could be. If you belonged to her, nobody or nothing could pry you out of her hands. He wished his first wife had been that way.

Ever since coming to Clifton, the children by his first marriage had been on his mind. Maybe it was because when they left him, Polly had moved them to Anderson, South Carolina. Her Papa had been in Tennessee working in mines when he had met her.

She had stayed with him when her parents went back home to South Carolina. He knew he had not been the best husband, but all he ever wanted to do was to make a living for his family.

If only he could see them! He hated he hadn't seen them grow up. Beck figured they never wanted to see his face again. They probably didn't remember him trying to come and get them that one time and him being beat out of the house with a broom by their mother. It was probably for the best that Polly had them, but he sure did wish they knew that he loved them. The ponderings of the last few days made them heavy on his mind, and he had dreamed about them last night.

Peter was always a Daddy's boy. Beck couldn't walk a step that his firstborn son wasn't trying to step in his Papa's footprints. It was hard to think that he might never see him again. You never could tell what Polly had told them about how she came to be in one state and him in another.

Beck left the house and walked up to Vinegar Hill and looked at the graves. He hadn't gone back to his mama's or papa's grave even after he and Lottie moved back to Tennessee. It was hard to think about losing them. Vinegar Hill and the Baptist Church where they were buried were the same in the fact that they were both on a hill above a river.

His papa had given Beck a love for the water, teaching him to fish and to swim the year he turned six. In the winter, they trapped beaver and minks on the banks of the Little Pigeon.

Beck wanted to be a Papa as good as his own. He felt like such a failure. Lottie had every right to be mad that he hadn't gone after the peeper. He should've been the one to protect his family. He'd ask around tomorrow and see if anyone else had the same problem with a peeper, and what could be done about it. No doubt somebody knew him. He was a pitiful excuse for a man to do such a thing.

***

Beck and Lottie sat on the porch on Sunday afternoon and looked over the mill town. Lottie had fixed him a soakie...a cup of coffee with a spoon of sugar and a biscuit crumbled up in the cup. Beck set the cup on the porch, laid his hand on his leg, and tapped on his knee. "I miss working with the seasons like we did on the farm. Here, its day in and day out, from sunrise to sunset, or the opposite if you're the night workers. On the farm, there was winter. It was a time we could rest and prepare for spring planting. There's no rest here. It's so loud in that mill you can't hear yourself think. I'm not sure I like public work. Every day, I leave choking on lint and dust. It's so hot and sweaty in there. Everything I work on is for someone else where the farm was all for my family. The pay is not enough to let any extra make it to the jar. Not enough can be saved to get out of here. Somebody gets sick, and we have to pay the doctor. We've had more sickness here than we ever did on the farm. These houses are too near one another. I'm homesick. I miss it where the closest you can tell someone lives near you is from the smoke coming out of the chimney in the winter or a wagon coming down the road. There was a rhythm to the farm. Seasons gave us time to rest, and rainy days help balance the hard labor of the fields. The pace here is set by big machines, and it never stops. It's steady and the speed is quick. The worst is I don't see many getting out of here. They keep us like slaves by providing houses and company pay."

Lottie wiped tears with her apron. "I know what you mean. I miss Mama and Papa. I want to see Sugar and the rest of my family. Letters ain't good enough. I want to see their face. Sugar wrote that Mama and Papa are looking old. They've probably changed so I wouldn't even know them if I seen 'em."

"I know you're homesick. We can't go back there for lots of reasons, even though I want to as bad as you. Your Papa understands.."

"You say that, but nobody tells me why we can't. I heard someone say in the company store the other day that they are building Lake Toxaway. It's near where Papa grew up. They're clearing land for the water in the lake to spread. You could work there."

"I'd still be working for somebody else. I want to work for myself."

"You ain't working for yourself here." Lottie wiped the tears from her jaw and went into the house.

"I know it, but here I can make enough money to buy land...a farm of my own." He yelled at her back.

"It doesn't seem like there'll ever be enough." She yelled back.

He took off his hat and pushed his hand over his sweaty forehead. He rubbed through his hair and slapped the hat back on his head. He hated that he had brought his family to such a place. They were not used to living like this.

The steps squeaked with his weight. Beck traipsed into the front yard and around back. There was room for a small garden like the company suggested they plant. He squatted down and took a stick and dug into the hard ground. Red sandy soil in his hand sifted through his fingers. If it could grow a crop, he'd be surprised. For one thing, it was as hard as a rock. Digging the dirt up without a horse and plow would jar a person's teeth out. But buying all their food from the store would take every penny they earned. Next year, they must grow some of it, and let Lottie store up for the winter. If they could grow cabbage, she could make kraut in the crock she'd brought with her.

Beck picked up a rock and threw it down the hill toward the road, folded his hands under his arm pits, and looked up toward the sky.

They had gone to the closest church this morning, which was Clifton Baptist Church. To be honest, Beck hadn't listened to much of the sermon today. He decided to take his communion with God here in the yard and bowed his head.

"Why can't I get ahead and provide for my family? I'm not going to leave this family and work away from them. I plan to have them with me. But what have I brought them into? To live in this disease infested village? To starve my family half to death to be able to get enough money to buy some land somewhere...maybe in Tennessee? Is this a bad desire? Does anybody up there really care if we live or die? We ain't never had nothing but trouble, Lottie or me. Give us a chance to make a good life for our family. I failed one wife and our children. Please, don't let me fail another."

***

There was a rumble of thunder, and Beck looked to the west where dark clouds were climbing up the sky and coming in the direction of Clifton. He kicked at the red dust. This would make horrible mud to carry into the house on the wood floors.

The three oldest were taking a nap. Lottie sat on the porch in the rocker. Her chin dropped to her chest as she dozed.

Beck had slept fitfully last night but couldn't nap when the sun was in the sky instead of the moon. He decided to walk near the river.

Laughter from children and adults alike drifted up to him as he got near the water. He stepped through a row of bushes and looked at the sand bank across the river by Dexter Mill where he worked. There were hundreds of people up and down the bank. Several couples sat on blankets or quilts together, talking and laughing. One young mother ran toward the river and dragged a toddler back with her close to her quilt. She sat him in the sand and gave the child sticks and a cup to play with. Older children played along the bank. Several were in the water.

The wind started to blow and women grabbed their hats. Many jumped up and took their quilt toward the bank that shielded them from the wind.

Near the dam, there were big rocks with young people, mostly in their teen years, sitting together and laughing. Some had paired off into couples and were certainly courting. One boy stood and bent his arm to an angle. The girls giggled and a pretty young redhead reached to feel his muscle. Another young man walked from rock to rock toward them, sporting a piece of straw between his teeth. He lay down on his side, and two girls went to sit near him. He recognized many from the mill. Others probably worked at one of the other mills.

He needed to persuade Lottie to bring the children and come down to the water some Sunday afternoon. It might bring her out of the mulley grubs she'd been in since they got here. She didn't like crowds much though, probably due to the fact she had grown up sheltered from people other than her own family. He wouldn't go down there by himself. He'd just wait until the whole family could go.

The river twisted and turned, deep in places and shallow in others. There were other sandy shores but none as big as where the people had gathered. He found a section of land by the water that was free from bushes and lay down on the ground and looked up at the sky. Life had not been what he had hoped for when he was like those young men, prancing and preening in front of the girls.

He dozed but a voice on the road above woke him. He didn't have a quilt and the damp sand had soaked his shirt. The clouds had left the horizon and were directly over him.

Beck backtracked and walked beside the river. Most of the merrymakers had gone home. He crossed the bridge over the dam to the Company Store.

***

The boy slipped to the side of the store and watched Beck. He leaned against the side and waited for Beck to come out. His brother had told him that he had seen the name of a man named Beckley Radford on an old list of new hires at the Dexter Mill in Clifton. He didn't believe him at first. After several weeks, he decided to come to see if it was true. There he was in flesh and blood.

Beck took his time looking through the company store. He reached his hand into his pocket and felt the pieces of paper that made up the coupon book. On the sheets were money marks, 25 cents, 5 cents, 2 cents, and 1 cent. The mill foreman had explained how he could go to the store and buy anything with them. They gave him some pay, but most his wages were to be given in these coupons.

He ran his fingers over the suit that hung on a frame from a nail in the dry goods sections. Beside it, there hung a woman's dress with flowers all over it. It would look good on Lottie. Speaking of her, she had given him a list of needed food staples. No need to dream of such finery now. It would be quite a while before they could afford more than food to eat and rent on the house. There would come a day when they could buy things like this, but not until they saved and got a place of their own.

Beck knew there was no use wallowing in all of his have-nots. He came out and sat on the steps of the store. He nodded at the young man that leaned against the side of the building with his hat pulled low over one side of his head and face.

Beck needed to take the coupon book back to Lottie, and let her get anything they might need. It all seemed very costly to him, but then again he never shopped much. He was hard put to know how this little amount of money and coupons could get enough food for all the workers in the family, much less other stuff they had in the store that was needed.

"Do you mind if I sit down beside you, mister?"

Without looking up, Beck answered, "Sure, go ahead. It's a free country, or so they tell me."

Beck put his elbows on his knees and crossed his arms across the span between them. He laid his forehead on his arms. He spit on the steps at his feet.

"Been here long, mister?"

Beck really didn't want to talk, but it might get his mind off his questioning his own sanity for coming to South Carolina. "A little over six months, long enough to wonder what made me think this was a good idea."

"So you don't like it in South Carolina?" When Beck didn't answer, the boy continued. "I live over in Spartanburg. I work at Mill Number One, and I take the trolley over there each morning. I live at home with my Mama and brother and two sisters."

Beck raised his head and looked at the boy. It didn't take him long to realize who he was. The eyes were like staring into a looking glass. The same angle of the jaw. The same dark, unruly, curly hair. "Peter?"

The boy took a deep breath and looked away. He stared down the road, like he was ready to run.

Beck laid his hand on the arm of the young man beside him. The boy looked down at his hand.

"Peter?"

"Yes. I'm Peter." The young man stood up, and Beck's hand dropped. He moved away from Beck.

"I thought y'all moved to Anderson, South Carolina."

"You mean you knew where we were and never came to see us, even when you were this close."

"You know I once tried to come and see you while you were still in Tennessee. Your Mama run me off and told me not to come back."

Beck stood up and went to stand near his son. "It's not that she didn't have a good reason to ask me to leave. I hadn't been the best husband or Papa. I was gone too much. If I could change things, I would. But that's not possible. I need to ask you to forgive me. I want to say I'm sorry."

Peter looked at Beck with tears on his eyes. "I remember a lot of things. Mama wouldn't have let you come back if you tried. That day you tried to visit us and she ran you off with a broom...I got so mad at Mama. I hated her. In spite of the way she talked about you to us, I knew all of it was not true. I planned someday to come and find you. It doesn't seem possible that I found you this close.

"She had every right to hate me, but I wish she hadn't talked about me like she did to you."

Beck nodded. "I asked her to stop, and she didn't do it again. She quit talking about you altogether."

***

No one slept well that night. Lottie dreamed that she and Sugar were running hand in hand...not in the mountains but through the graves at Vinegar Hill. They then raced each other to the river. They were young girls again.

Beck dreamed about the mountains. He walked on ground that he knew he finally owned, perhaps a hundred acres or more. It was so peaceful. He walked all the way around the outside edges of his land. In his hand, he held the deed. As he came to the bottom land near a creek, a group of men saw him. One man yelled something at Beck and pointed in his direction. He awoke as they ran toward him, and he sat up in the bed.

Beck laid back and closed his eyes. It had felt good to be in the mountains. So real! The wind blew through the trees and whipped at his back. He had heard dogs hunting in the distance, barking as they treed a 'coon. Squirrels jumped from tree to tree and chattered at him. How he would love to go back!

Beck guessed he'd never again see Jackson County. Other mountains just wouldn't be the same, not even those of East Tennessee. He felt like an outcast, always meant to walk with strangers and people that did not know him or his family...not who they really were at any rate. People were different from place to place, as well as land. Town dwellers were not like mountain people. Oh, how he missed folks from the country.

Chapter 11

August 1901

"A Wednesday's child is full of woe," said the midwife as she wrapped the baby boy and laid him in Lottie's outstretched arms.

"But it's only a few minutes after midnight, barely even Wednesday. I should have pushed harder early on." Lottie lay still and looked at her baby boy. The midwife cleared the rags and sheets from the birth. She took them to the wash water that she had had Beck heat in the wash pot.

The baby whimpered, and Lottie put him to her breast to feed him. "Hush little one. It's close enough to midnight that I'll say your birthday is Tuesday, August 27, 1901. You won't be a child of woe but full of grace. I shall name you Tolliver Beckley Radford."

"Call his date of birth what you will, but he'll still be a child of woe. You can't change anything by playing like it didn't happen." The midwife pushed her supplies into the bag she had brought with her and went out the door.

***

Lottie turned to her right side and pulled Tolliver over to her other breast. It was good to lay in the quietness and watch her baby. Florence had the other children. Lottie told her to send them home by daybreak so they could get ready to go to work.

Beck came in the door. "Lottie, I took the granny woman home. I didn't have time to let you know much more than her name. She's the one that the other women at the mill said they used. She did her job, I see."

Beck sat down on the edge of the bed and wrapped the baby's fingers around his own little finger. "He's so tiny."

Lottie laughed. "It's a good thing, but I don't consider him too small. The midwife said about eight pounds. If he'd been any bigger, I don't think I would've been able to have him. It took a lot out of me."

Beck stared at his son. "If'n he's through eating, I'll hold him a bit and let you sleep."

There was a smile on Lottie's pale lips. "He's yours...go ahead and take him."

He slipped his hands under the bundle and brought the baby to his chest. "Sleep if you can. I brought in the rocker from the porch. There are only a few hours until work time, so I will hold him until then."

Lottie took a deep breath and turned her back to them.

***

Beck listened to Lottie's even, quiet breaths. He took the baby from his shoulder and laid him in his lap. He looked at his tiny face and whispered his name.

He thought of Peter. Beck knew how hard it had been to lose his own papa as a man. It had to be harder on a young boy to lose his. He knew he should have tried harder to find work nearby and stay home. But bygones were bygones, and there was nothing he could do about it now. He now needed to be a good Papa to Tolliver and to Lottie's children. They didn't have a papa other than him. He'd be the one they remembered. It wouldn't make up for losing his first family by being a better father to his new family, but it would be wise to use his experiences to do better.

Beck took Tolliver's tiny hand and wrapped it around his finger. "You are mine and Lottie's first baby together."

The trolley passed and bells rang. Lottie opened her eyes and listened to Beck talk to their baby.

The baby made a sucking sound in his sleep and Beck smiled. "You have brothers and sisters right here in the house that'll help tend to you, but I want you to know that you have other family too. Two brothers and two sisters, Peter and Billy, Sarah and Maude. I ain't been much of a Papa to your brothers and sisters. Your big brother, Peter, might get to see you soon. If the others forgive me for all the things I've done, you might get to see them, too. I'll make sure I tell Peter all about you when I see him Sunday."

Lottie choked as she listened to Beck talk to his son. "What are you talking about? You know where your children are? You've been seeing them on the side without telling me?"

Beck turned toward Lottie. She faced him and was crying.

"Why would you do that, Beck? How did you find them? And, mostly, WHY would you look for them and not tell me?"

Beck brought the baby and laid him beside Lottie. "I didn't look for them. They found me by chance. The only thing I knew was that they moved to South Carolina to be near her family."

"Is that why you brought us to Clifton...so you could be near them, near to Polly, your first wife?" Tears rolled down her cheeks.

"I never thought about them being near here until we were on the train coming down. Even then, I didn't think I'd see them. It just happened. One day I'm at the store, and Peter comes up to me. I realized who he was pretty quick. One of the boys had seen my name on a list of new workers at the Dexter Mill. Peter came to see if it was really me. I try to see him about every two weeks on a Sunday. We'll meet at the store over by Dexter or down by the river. He works at Mill Two."

"So you've been lying to me when you take those Sunday walks to rest your mind, you say. Does Polly meet you, too?"

Beck came to the side of the bed. "No! I've not seen the others yet. Peter has told Billy, Sarah, and Maude about me living close. He's not told his mother anything so far. Not that he needs to. She doesn't have to know. She never wanted me to see them again and said as much the last time I saw her."

Lottie pulled Tolliver close and turned them both to face the wall. She touched the tiny face and caused it to turn to her bare breast. His tongue popped against the roof of its mouth as he tried to suckle before he took a good hold.

"I didn't try to hide this from you. It was time for the baby to be born, and I didn't want to trouble you. I would've told you soon."

The knock at the door was Florence. She had a pan of gravy that she held with several layers of rags. Behind her was Annie May with a bowl of hot biscuits

"I've got your children and breakfast. What was the baby?"

Lottie turned her head to Florence. "It's a boy. I named him Tolliver."

Beck looked over Lottie at the baby. "Tolliver. I like that."

"I named him Tolliver Beckley." Lottie stared at her husband. "After his Papa. I guess it's the first one that carries his given name. Is it, Beck?"

Beck looked sideways at Florence and then back toward Lottie. "It is." He turned around to the children. "You all need to eat fast, and let's get to work. If any of us are late, it can hurt us all."

***

The smell of collards cooking drifted through the open window. Lottie opened the back door, walked down the steps, and stood in the yard. The door to Oliver and Novella Findley's side of the house stood open. A child laughed in another room of their house. There was a clatter that sounded like a pot fell. As that ended, there was a scream from Novella Findley, and she fell out the door toward Lottie. There was collard greens splattered over her arms and stuck to her dress. Her arms were red and blistered.

"Novella, get off the dress as quick as you can. It's holding that boiling water against your skin."

She jumped to her feet.

When Lottie jumped, she almost fell out of the bed. Tears streamed down her face, and she shook so hard the bed creaked.

"What's going on?" Beck rolled over.

"It was a bad dream. I'm fine now. Go back to sleep. You only have another hour to sleep before getting up time."

Beck turned his back to her. Lottie lay still until she heard him snoring then slipped out of the bed and to the table.

What am I going do? Do I *tell the hateful old woman she's going to be burned by boiling collard water or let it happen without a warning?* Lottie put her hand on her jaw and looked out at the last moonlight of the morning. Novella had a choice to cook the collards, and it probably couldn't wait. Lottie had watched the early collards mature in Novella's little garden at the back of the house, and they were now ready to pick. It could happen any time. *Is it worth my time to warn some hag that hates my guts and won't believe a word I say? It would serve her right if I didn't for the way she treats my family.*

Her Papa's words spoke near her ear. 'Just because everybody else is mean don't give you the right to do the same.'

"Hush up Papa. You ain't here, and you have no idea what kind of person she is." Lottie said aloud.

There was no more time to think about it. The faint glow in the east meant she had better get a fire burning and ready for cooking.

***

Lottie would clean a little. Then, she'd stop and walk back and forth from the table to the door. If she was going to do something, it had to be soon. Novella had picked the collards right after daylight.

Beck and the children had been at work for nearly an hour when Lottie smelled the collards cooking. She peeked out the back door and saw Novella lean over a tin tub to push the leaves deep into the water. The pot to her side was full of more greens. A small pot had some ready for boiling for dinner that day.

The saying that you should never tell a dream until a week after you have it was not possible this time. Either way, it was going to come true it seemed.

Novella picked up the pot and turned toward Lottie. "Why are you staring at me? Don't you have work to do?"

Lottie curved her lips in a tight, crooked smile. "I have plenty to do. I thought I ought to tell you something. I think it's the right thing to do."

"Well, spit it out. The day's a-wasting."

It was the hardest time that Lottie could remember trying to talk politely with someone. "I had a dream about you last night."

"A dream about me? Why would you dream about me?" She laughed when she looked at Lottie's red face.

"It might be best if you know that my dreams come true most of the time. Back in North Carolina, they called me the sighted sister. I wouldn't be telling you this unless I think you're in danger. I can't promise it will happen just like I saw it."

"Danger? Hmp. What kind of trouble could come my way?"

Lottie stared at the pot in Novella's hand. "The collards you're going to cook on the stove...you need to be careful..."

"You're as crazy as I first thought. Tend to your own business, and I'll do the same." She laughed and went into the house.

It was just after quitting time at the mill when Lottie heard the scream next door. She ran outside in time to see Novella fall out onto the porch. Lottie started to go to her when Oliver's foot hit the first step. His hands scraped the collard leaves from his wife's arms. He ripped the upper portion of her dress as he pulled it from her scalded body.

He swept Novella up into his arms and carried her inside. A few minutes later, one of the children left running. Within the hour, the doctor arrived.

Beck, Lottie, and the children ate supper in silence, listening to Novella scream in pain from time to time. The doctor left, but the crying and screams went on all night.

The next morning Lottie knocked on the door before Oliver left for work.

"I'm sorry about the accident with your wife."

Oliver nodded. 'Come in. She's there on the bed if you want to say a word to her. That's our married daughter, Elsie, beside her."

Lottie walked over and put a hand on the bedpost. “Miss Novella, I’m real sorry about your burns. If there is anything I can do…”

Novella stared at Lottie then turned her face to the wall without speaking.

Elsie reached her hand out and covered Lottie’s.

Oliver said, “I’m real sorry she won’t speak to you. She’s been in a right smart of pain through the night…”

Lottie spoke before he could finish. “We heard her crying.”

Oliver turned red. “I guess you did.” He looked at his children standing by the door. “I’m leaving one of the boys here today to watch after her and the baby. Thank you for stopping by.”

Lottie left without another word.

***

Lottie cooked twice as much of everything when she fixed meals for her family. She placed a pot of something…beans, vegetable soup, or such…by the Finley’s door, knocked hard, and ran back into the house. The next day, the pot would be by her door, empty, and washed clean. Yet, neither the Findleys nor the Radfords ever spoke during that time.

Chapter 12

August 1901

"That's it! I'm going to stop this once and for all." Beck came inside after chopping up kindling for the cook stove to use the following week. "They've stolen the last stick of wood from me."

"Are they still taking it?" Lottie wiped her hands on her apron.

"Yes…I counted the sticks last night, and there are four missing. They try to take just a little bit each time, thinking I won't miss it. I've thought about it, and I know exactly what I'm going to do."

"What's that?" Lottie watched him pull out a hand drill from the box of tools behind the cook stove. He stopped by the cabinet and dipped out some lard with a spoon. He sat down and began to drill.

"Just hide and watch. It won't take but a day or two until we know exactly who's the thief."

Brody sat down beside his Papa and watched.

"Get me the gunpowder, son. "Brody jumped up and brought him the can of gunpowder. He watched as Beck packed the holes chunk full of the powder. Beck took a finger and packed lard into the top of the holes.

After all the things were put away, Beck stacked the wood onto Brody's arms, and they went outside to place them back on the top of the woodpile.

"Now, we'll wait and see," he said.

***

Peter stretched out on the grass beside the trolley stop. His Papa had not been on the last one, but he would wait for the next one from Clifton that should arrive in thirty minutes. He bent his elbows. One arm was under this head, and he laid the other across his upper face. He jumped when his arm touched the bruise above his left eye.

He had tried to get Billy and Sarah to come with him. They had said no, but had not ruled out coming sometime to meet him. Papa was not as bad as his Mama had said. Well, at least now he wasn't. The memory of his Papa being at home was foggy. There had been no arguing that he remembered, but a right smart of time his Papa was gone.

He must have dozed, as the next thing he remembered was a bell clanging and Beck standing over him.

"Hello, Son. Glad you got a nap. Sorry I'm late. I had a few things to take care of at home, but I wouldn't have missed this time for anything."

Peter smiled. "I knew you'd come, so I waited."

"The others didn't come like I hoped?" Beck looked around.

"No. I think they will some other day. By and large, they ain't dead set against it…just taking their time."

Peter reached up and touched his face. Beck saw the black eye and the cut above Peter's left eye.

"What happened to you?" A pulse throbbed at Beck's temples. Beck had said it so loud that others stopped to look their way.

"Let's go down the street a ways to talk." Beck put his hand on Peter's shoulder.

Peter stopped at a grassy area at the edge of a large home belonging to a prominent Spartanburg family. He sat down and motioned for Beck to do the same. "I had a run-in with a man at the boarding house Mama operates. There are four men that live with us. It's the only way she can make ends meet. I'm planning on moving out as soon as I can. It'll make things harder on her, but it'll be better on me. I don't know that I can stop the next time until I've killed someone."

"Peter! What happened?"

"The man had pushed Mama against the wall. She slapped him as I came in the door. He laughed at her. I grabbed him and threw him on the floor. He jumped up and caught me off guard. He got one good lick in." Peter pointed at his eye. "But that was the only one. The others had to pull me off of him."

"Is your Mama alright?"

"She's fine. It makes me mad that she won't make the man move out. She says she needs the money. There are others that would jump to get his room, but she acts like she's afraid they won't. I hope that's the only reason she lets him stay. She acts all prissy in front of him, and I hate it. That might be the reason she won't make him leave. I'm going to tell her it's either him or me. One of us has to go."

Beck put his elbow on his knee, and his hand stroked his forehead. "Do you want me to go down there and take care of this?"

Peter laughed. "No. I think you ought not be within a broom handle's distance of Mama. Maybe just a little further than a gunshot length would be better. She's not keen on you. She found out that I've been meeting you. It made her as mad as a hornet, yet she asked a lot of questions...about what you looked like now and other things about you."

Beck said, "I want you and the others to know I'm sorry. It's not all my fault, but neither is it all your Mama's either. I care a lot about each one of you."

Peter watched his Papa look into the distance like he was remembering another place or time. For a long time, he was not really there with him. Peter waited.

Beck said, “I want to come to see her and the others the next time we meet. Is that agreeable with you?”

“I don’t think it’s a good idea, but I’ll be there with you, if that’s what you’re going to do.”

A big grin spread over Beck’s face. “I’d like that just fine. That’s all a man could ask.”

***

It was early the next morning, and Lottie had put lard in the pan to make gravy. Beck put on his shoes and tied them. A sound, near as loud as a cannon, went off. It was at a house two streets below them, and smoke curled out. Both hurried out on the porch as did nearly everyone within a quarter mile. There was coughing and sputtering from all the members of the household as they ran from the building and into the streets.

“Wheehooo.” Beck shouted to the top of his voice. “Now we know. Let that be a lesson to you. Guess somebody will need to buy a new cookstove now that they blew the top off.”

“Hush. They’ll know who put the powder in the wood.” Lottie wrung her hands and popped her knuckles.

"I hope they do know. Not only do they know who put in the gunpowder, we also know who stole the wood!"

"Beck!"

"Be sure your sins will find you out," he yelled.

Chapter 13

August 1901

Lottie waited until a night when there was no moon. She sat on the porch and waited for the lamps in windows all around to go out.

The six chickens... one rooster and five hens... clucked lightly as she pushed open the door to the hen house and stepped high. Her foot caught on one of the limbs Beck had put in the hen house for the chickens to perch upon. The rooster lost its footing and fell to the ground. He hopped back onto his roosting site, and Lottie sat down on the ground in the corner. She brushed away dirt, pulled up a glass jar, and poked a dab of money inside. *A little more money stashed away.* There was the flour barrel jar, but this one was special.

What Lottie really wanted was to go home. She had written her Papa and had asked if he would give them land and help them build a house if they came back. He hadn't written, but she knew the letter would come any day. It might be wishful thinking that she might get to go home, but she prayed every day she would. Soon she was going to talk to Beck about it...when there was more money in the hen house jar.

***

A few days later, Lottie's homesickness reached a peak.

"Beck, please, let's go back to Jackson County. Papa will give us land and help us build a home. Owen is dead."

The anger on Beck's face spilled into his voice. "We can't go there," he yelled. "I've told you before that it wouldn't be wise. Too much has happened. We need to stay here where we can make more money. Someday we can go to Tennessee and buy land. We'll live there. That is if we can save some money."

Lottie bit her lip. "I've started saving a little here and there. I have my own jar where I put money. One that doesn't leak like the other one seems to be doing. I try to save up a dozen eggs every two weeks and sell to the store, and then put that money back."

Beck looked down into Lottie's eyes. "Some of those times that we only had sawmill gravy and biscuits for breakfast, you had saved the eggs and sold them?"

She swallowed hard. “That’s true, but only on a Sunday. I wouldn’t let you all work hard and not have eggs for breakfast. You needed your strength on work days.” She watched his face. “I got the money hid in the henhouse in a jar.”

Beck’s eyes grew large. “How much do you have?”

“Nowhere near enough yet, but it’s a start. I want to get my babies out of this pest-ridden town. If one person take’s a sniffle, everyone else is coughing and sneezing within the week…the fever or other illnesses spread even quicker. Please help me take them back to the mountains. The air is clean and fresh there.”

“Don’t let nobody see you hiding that money. I heard a tale that people stole money from a man at the mill that hid his under his back step. They saw him putting it there and dug it up that night, they think.”

“I only do it on the dark of the moon, after everyone else is in bed. The chickens don’t hardly cluck anymore when I come in and out, they’s so used to me. Can we go back to Papa’s? Please.”

Beck rubbed the back of his neck. “We’ll think about it. Let’s get the money first and see what happens.”

“Beck, we’re stuck to this mill as tight as bark on a tree. We’ll never have anything of our own if we stay here. Our children will be the same. Our lives are tangled and tied up into these jobs for better or worse like a marriage. They have us like a prisoner with a house and company coupon books."

Beck sat down at the table. He leaned his chair back until it sat on the two back legs, and the ladder back rested against the wall behind him. His head lay against the wall. He put both hands over this face, and pushed them up and over his dark hair.

"Lottie, I know there ain't nothing but poor people here, but I have a plan to save all we can to get us out. The one thing I know is that it's a guaranteed pay check and a roof over our head as long as we can work. Try to think about all the things it gives the children. They have friends close, and they can visit with them every day. We have to make the most of our time whilst we're here."

Lottie sat down across from him. "You may think about all it has given, but I ponder on all it's taken. How long do we have to stay? When can we get enough money to leave? I know there are some good things about living in a town, but it's hard to think of what they are when people get sick all around you, and children die. Our children."

Beck sat the chair back on all four legs. "Sickness came to homes when we lived in the mountains, too. This is nothing new."

"I know that's true, but not like it is here. The diseases kill hundreds at a time. Up on Vinegar Hill there are about a hundred new graves since we've come here, and that's just one of the graveyards in Clifton. There are more. It's sad how many graves cover that hill. Many don't even have a tombstone at the head. Just an old field rock, but the ground is fresh dug on some, and others have only been there long enough to settle with the rains. Most are little short graves. Ours included. He don't have a headstone. I want Sheffield's name at his head."

"When we get enough money to leave, I'll make sure that there's enough to either get a rock made, or I'll chisel it myself. I know it's important to you." Beck put his hands on the edge of the table and pulled his tired body out of the chair. "Try not to worry about that for now. There's too much other stuff to take care of. We know he's there and, before we're gone, we'll let everyone know we left a part of us here."

Lottie threw her apron over her head and cried softly. Beck watched her for a minute and walked out the door.

***

Wind whipped up the river and picked up Lottie's dress as she crossed the bridge near the store. She had left soon after Beck and the children left for work. She sold three dozen eggs to the storekeeper. It was near the railroad tracks on her way home when she saw the same buggy and the same two men that she had seen the day she met Florence. It rushed by her. The driver stood and beat the horses with a whip to make them speed up. The train came down the track closer and closer. They were trying to beat the train before it crossed in front of them and delayed their progress. It would be close. The horse balked just short of the tracks but jumped onto them as the whip came down on his back. The train hit them from the side and she saw the men flying through the air. Before they hit the ground, the vision was gone.

"Are you alright, madam?" The man grabbed her arm before she slid to her knees in weakness.

"I'm just a little weak at the knees. Thank you for catching me, but I'll be just fine."

"Are you sure? I can get someone to help me, and we'll get you home."

Lottie shook her head hard from side to side. "I'll be just fine. You can be on your way."

The man shrugged his shoulders. "Whatever you say."

Lottie made it to the Methodist church and plopped down on the top step. This time, she had recognized the man driving the buggy as Florence's husband. The man beside him was not anyone she'd seen before, but he had a doctor's bag in his lap to which he was holding onto for dear life.

Lottie looked up toward their houses. "Do I tell her what I've seen? If so, will she believe me?" She laid her arms across her knees and put her head down. *If only this horrible ability would go away. It's useless to know something if you can't change what's going to happen. I don't even know when it's going to happen. Why did they need a doctor?*

The hill seemed steeper today than ever. She must go by Florence's house, but she didn't know what to say.

***

Florence stood on the front porch and held to the posts. She heaved and vomited. Her forehead fell against her arm, and she groaned. "I'm so sick. I've never been so sick in all my life."

Lottie helped her to a chair and rubbed her hair back from her eyes. "I'll get a rag and wet it." She brought it back to Florence. "What brought this on?"

Theirs eyes met, and Florence smiled. "I think you already know the answer to that."

"You're in the family way?"

"Yep. I'd say about two months along if all the signs I've been noticing are anything to go by." She laughed.

Lottie felt chill bumps go over her arms. She knew now why they might need a doctor in a few months. There was now no way she could tell Florence about the sight she had seen.

"Will you be alright? Has the sickness passed?

Florence stood. "I'll be fine now that I don't have to cook until the afternoon. The smell of food makes me queasy. Ooo-wee, how long does this sickness last?"

"It's different with every baby. Eat a bite before you get up in the morning. If you feel sick, lie down. Take care of yourself. I've got to get back to the house." Lottie waved and rushed home. The vision made her uneasy, and she wasn't ready to talk about it with her friend yet.

Chapter 14

August 1901

The store had cleared of people from their morning shopping when Lottie arrived. She carried Tolliver in a sheet she had tied around her neck in a sling that held him against her. She would need both hands for shopping.

"I have a letter for you, Misses Radford."

"For me?" Lottie put up both hands and covered her mouth. "Are you sure?"

The man smiled. "It says Mrs. Lottie Radford. That's you, right?

Lottie smiled, and her face lit up. "It sure is. I haven't had a letter in months. I'm just excited, that's all."

"Letters from family are a wonderful thing. I take it's from family."

Lottie tore open the envelope and looked at the last page. "It sure is. It's from my Mama. Thank you much."

"Sure. That's what I'm here for."

"I'll be back for my bill of groceries as soon as I read this."

Lottie rushed to the edge of the river, found a rock, and sat down. She swept all the sticks from the grass beside her and laid both Tolliver and the sheet beside her. It was good that the baby was asleep. She wanted some peace to read her letter. She carefully opened it and read aloud.

> *Dearest daughter, we are doing fine and hope you are the same. This year has been hard on your Papa, but he is doing better now that the crops are in. We talked about you and the children last night, and it made me want to see you. I miss you something awful. So does the rest of the family, your Papa included although he tries not to show it. Mostly to keep me from fretin' about it, I think. Sugar came in while we were talking about you. She has decided to come there and visit. I offered to take care of all her concerns if she'd come and see about you. I couldn't because I can't leave your Papa. We figured she was the best one to come. You two were always closer than the others. She's next to the best thing of me being there. I hope that's true for you, too.*

Two women dressed in fine clothes passed her. They were probably wives of some of the visitors from the owners of the mill that lived in Spartanburg. She looked up as they went by. They nodded their heads but immediately looked at each other and raised their eyebrows. Lottie watched until they were well past her, at which time one reached over and whispered to the other.

She read a bit more but this time to herself. Tolliver whimpered and she began to read aloud in hopes her voice would soothe him back to sleep.

I never thought my family would live so far away from me. It's hard for me to understand why you couldn't come home once Owen was gone, but your Papa says its best. He just won't explain why it has to be like that. It has always seemed he was right, so I must trust him for this, too.

Take care of my sweet babies that it seems I may never meet this side of heaven. They're a part of you Lottie, so they mean a lot to me, even if I never lay eyes on them.

Love, Mama

Oh yes, I forgot to say that Sugar will be there next week by train. I'll wire the time. She goes to Asheville then down to Spartanburg. Meet her, if you're able.

Her dream was coming true. It was a good sign for a change.

***

Lottie paced up and down the wooden platform and, once in a while, would lean out and look down the tracks. The train was late. According to the big clock hanging on the wall above the ticket office, it was only twenty minutes past time, but it seemed like hours. It had been almost two years since she'd seen Sugar. If only her Papa and Mama could have come she would have been completely content. They were too old and sick to make the trip. Lottie knew they'd not been well for some time. Even though Beck had halfway promised, there was never enough money left over for a train ticket for her and the children to go. Neither was there money to send to her papa and mama to come see her.

Lottie watched as people pushed off the train, running here and there and meeting family. People hugged, and there were happy tears.

"Lottie." Sugar grabbed Lottie in a bear hug. "I'm so glad to be here. That there train is hotter than Mama's garden in early August. Who'd believe this is almost September with this heat? It's also smelly in there, what with the smoke and hot people all pushed into it."

Sugar watched a big smile dance on Lottie's lips. "Are you laughing at me?"

"I'm just so glad to see you and hear your voice. I can hear you giving them a piece of your mind all the way from Asheville. I wish I was as outspoken as you." Lottie hugged her tightly again and stepped back. She looked at Sugar from head to toe then grabbed her around the waist and hugged her hard. "I miss you so very much."

"Don't squeeze me in two, sister girl. You were teasing about that outspoken part, right? I remember your letters about how you don't mind speaking up for yourself or the children."

Lottie laughed until people turned to watch them. She turned red at the stares, but Sugar waved off their attention. "They have no idea how long it's been since we've seen each other. I can't wait to see your babies. Bet they've grown a foot."

"Sheffield ain't with us no more, you know."

Sugar stuck out her lower lip, and tears filled her eyes. "I'm so sorry sister. I did know. I can't imagine what you felt when you had to put him away."

"I do have a new baby. His name is Tolliver. He's mine and Beck's first baby together. Beck just loves that baby to death. He picks him up the minute he comes in the house after work." Lottie's face glowed. "You have to see him. He sure is a pretty baby. Not that the others were ugly," she laughed, "but he has the perfect little, round head and a head full of hair. The others were bald."

They hugged again. Each grabbed a bag and walked to the trolley that would take them to Clifton.

"These bags are heavier than rocks. What have you got in them?"

"Mama sent you some cans of food and some taters. I wrapped those jars in my dresses so they didn't rattle or break."

Lottie stared at the bags. "Mama sure is good to me. I miss her so bad. I wish we could move back there, but Beck says that we can make more money here. He plans to buy a farm somewhere when we get money put back for it. I sure hope its back in Jackson County."

Sugar's eyes grew round, and she raised her eyebrows. "That might not be best, sister. You go wherever Beck wants to take you." She leaned closer to Lottie's ear. "Too much has happened there."

"Oh Sugar, Owen is dead, and he can't hurt me no more. His family will only pretend I ain't there. They never did care for me anyway. I need my family in a bad way. I don't need either farm or money. I only want to come home and live where you all are. I'll take in washing or do whatever I have to do to make money, when we need it. I also heard a tale that they're building a dam and making Lake Toxaway, and that there are all kinds of hotels and eating places going up for rich people from Asheville to go for the summer and be on the lake. I know that Beck could get a job there. I told him so. I know..."

"Stop it Lottie. You can't come back. You need to listen to your husband, and forget that notion."

Sugar looked at the others on the trolley that had leaned in toward them to listen to the women talk. The clanging noise on the tracks had caused them to talk much too loud. "Let's not talk about this until these eavesdroppers are gone." She spoke this loud on purpose so they *would* hear.

The next stop was Glendale. The trolley creaked to a standstill, and people pushed to get off and into the cooler air. Lottie turned to her sister, and tears came up in Lottie's eyes. "Don't you want me to come back home? Don't Mama and Papa want me? I know I left my first husband, and that was a sin. I left with Beck. It was to save my life and my children's. Owen was mean to me. He was a terrible person. Surely everybody can forgive me, now that he's gone and I've done right."

Sugar pushed her sweaty hair back and pulled out a hairpin. She pushed it back in against the curly strays and fastened them to the ball of hair on top of her head. "Mama would be more than happy if you came back. She says all the time, 'It ain't natural all this moving they're doing.' She don't understand leaving land and family behind. But you do know that Owen's death was thought to be more than a natural death, don't you? Surely, Beck told you that."

Lottie grabbed a bag in each hand and stepped off. She waited for Sugar to come to her side. She frowned. "I don't know what you mean. How did he die? I guess I thought he just got sick and passed away. Was he killed? Why would Beck know?"

"Which one is your house amongst all these?" Sugar looked at the hill in front of her and frowned. "Where are the dad-blamed trees?"

Lottie pointed up to the top of the hill. "My house is up there on the back side. It's a steep hill, but it's nice. I can see over the others, and there's some land behind us that is not settled as heavy. It keeps me from feeling so crowded in on every side. There are a few trees near the graveyard. They used the trees on the hillside to build the houses."

"Lord Almighty! Papa and Mama would have a conniption fit if they knew you were living in a place like this."

Lottie spoke over her shoulder to Sugar. "You're not getting by with starting something like you have about Owen and not finishing it. Tell me how he died. I've never asked anybody. I was just so glad he was gone, and I never had to worry about him again."

Both women stopped and gasped for air about half way up and caught their breath. Before Lottie picked up her bag, she got in front of Sugar and put both hands on her hips. "You ain't answered my questions. You have me worried sick."

Sugar puckered her lips. "You always were a worry wart. Nothing gets past you. Did you know that Beck was back in our part of the country a few days before Owen died?"

"I know he had to go to Waynesville and pick up something for the farm boss. I didn't know he went to Jackson County. So, he came to see you?"

Sugar sat down her bags. “He did come to our house once, and everyone around the county knew it. He talked to Papa, and then he and I had a short pow-wow. There was speculation that maybe Owen was poisoned.”

“What? Do they think Beck poisoned Owen? Why would he want to do that? We were already gone. He didn’t have any reason to want him dead...”

Sugar shook her head to disagree. “Except that he could finally marry you if Owen was dead. It was common knowledge that Owen had been pestering you at two different places in Tennessee. So much so, that you all had to move to stay away from him. Beck did tell us you were expecting a child. He needed to marry you.”

Lottie turned red. She had not told her Mama that she was with child that early, and she had not told Sugar in any letters that she knew. “How did they know that he had followed us to Tennessee?”

Sugar turned and picked up her bag. “I guess that fool Owen bragged about it. How should I know? His side of the story would not have put you or Beck in a good light.”

Lottie was quiet for the rest of the walk to the house. She showed Sugar around their home, all the time with a frown on her face. “Beck, Brody, and Annie May are all at work. They work twelve hours a day, six days a week. August is at school. She works part of the time and goes to school some days.”

"Those babies work in a mill? They're too young to work."

"We couldn't have as many rooms in the house if they didn't. You must have a worker for each room you have. Otherwise, you get a smaller house. Beck wanted us to have a big house. I wanted to work, but he said the babies needed me more. It's hard, but they seem to get by tolerable with the hard labor. They have friends that work with them, and they have a good time while they work, at least when the foreman ain't standing over their shoulder. Anyways, that's what they tell me."

The sisters sat down at the kitchen table. "Sugar, do **you** think Beck killed Owen?"

Sugar looked away from Lottie and stared toward the door. "What makes you ask such a question? Just because Beck was there..."

Lottie leaned to the side and situated herself between Sugar's eyes and the door. "Look at me! Until now, I hadn't dreamt Beck could hurt even a flea. But you're scaring me with your stories about Owen's death. I do know that Beck was gone for several days on that trip, but he rode up just after the telegram came. Don't see how he could have beat a telegram back if he was the one that killed him. Then, again, I don't know the day Owen actually died. And if'n he was poisoned, he could have laid for days while Beck was coming back to me. I don't like to think he could have done such a thing. He hated what Owen did to me... to us... but we were away from there. There was no reason to go back to kill him." Lottie frowned. "What makes them think it was poison?"

With both elbows on the table and her chin resting on her fists, Sugar said, "He'd been living in town at the back of his mama and papa's store. They said he'd been feeling poorly for about a week with his belly hurting. That morning, his Mama cooked some cabbage. They said Owen ate a good helping. An hour later, he bent double with pain and took to his bed. He was dead before the day was out. The law came out and asked us about Beck, but we didn't say that we'd seen him that week. Papa acted like he didn't know where you were living. He told him about how Owen had chased you around until you were forced to not tell anyone where you were living. We did say that we were pretty sure you all were living in Tennessee. They dropped the matter as far as we know, but not before half the county got wind of it. It's been whispered all over the county from one gossip's lip to another person's itching ears ever since.

It was quiet for some time, each one dwelling on their own thoughts.

***

Annie May, August, and Brody raced up the hill like it was flat ground.

"Mama, did Aunt Sugar come on the train." August yelled before she could open the door.

Sugar ran out the door and scooped up August in her arms. Annie May grabbed her around the waist and pulled her to the rocker on the porch. Both girls sat on her lap. Brody looked at Sugar and smiled.

"Come here young man. You're not too old to hug your aunt."

Brody hugged Sugar with tears in his eyes.

"Oh, Brody. I miss you, too."

He wiped his eyes and sat down in the floor at her feet.

"They tell me you're not going to school. I don't think I like that."

Annie May stood up. "We're needed to work. Besides, you and Mama taught us to read before we went to school. We're smarter than the others anyway."

"Stop bragging." Brody pointed at his sister.

"There's more to school than just reading. I wish you all **could** come home. We have a new school house nearby."

August hugged Sugar. "I wish we could too, but Papa says we have to work really hard and not complain. If we do, someday we'll own land and not have to work in a mill anymore."

"As long as it's in a place with trees."

Lottie looked around. "I agree with you, buddy."

CHAPTER 15

September 1901

Do I tell her, or not? Lottie walked to the back door, changed her mind, and walked back to the table and sat down. She drummed her fingers on the table.

She rubbed her neck and recalled the vision she had again a few days ago...the buggy, Fate, the doctor, the train. It would not go away.

Lottie jumped up and the chair fell backwards.

Sugar was on the porch rocking Tolliver. "I have to go next door for something. I'll be back in a bit." She marched quickly to her friend's house.

At her home, Florence put her purse on her arm and closed the front door. She whirled around and came face to face with Lottie.

“I need to talk to you.” Lottie pulled Florence to the steps and sat down.

“What’s wrong? Are you sick?”

“I’m fine. It’s not about me.” Lottie said. “It’s about you, and about Fate, and the doctor…and the baby I think.”

“The baby?” Florence grabbed her belly. “Is something wrong?”

“Let me tell you what I saw, and we’ll talk about it.” Lottie told her everything, both what she saw the day at the cemetery and how the events were more clear when she had the vision near the bridge and railroad.

Florence folded her hands like she was praying and pulled them near her mouth. “Do you think something is going to happen to Fate? Will it come to pass no matter what we do, or can we can stop it?”

Lottie bit her lip. “I don’t know. I’ve never had a dream or vision that I thought I could stop from happening. It might have for Novella, if she would have listened. There’s no way to know for sure. If things didn’t happen in the order that it did in the dream, it might change the outcome. I pray we can stop it.”

Florence reached and pulled Lottie up. They stood face to face. “Thank you for telling me. I know it couldn't have been easy coming over and telling me my husband or the doctor might be killed."

Lottie hugged Florence. "I know it don't seem right to come and tell you this without thinking about ways to stop it. It'll worry you sick. I should've stayed home."

"No! You shouldn't have. I don't know what will happen, but I'm still glad you told me. Don't you worry about me. There was a reason, and I'll figure out what I'm to do with this sign from God. I believe that's what it is and that I'll know what to do when it's time."

***

The rain had left the air feeling clean and fresh. The showers cooled the hot days only for a short time.

The family had attended church together the last two Sundays. She liked the new church Beck had chosen to attend since Sheffield's funeral. The people seemed kind.

"Lottie, slow down. Why are you in such a rush?" Sugar pulled on Lottie's arm.

"I want to show you something." Lottie grabbed Sugar's hand.

"Does it have to be this minute? Can we walk slower so we can talk?"

Lottie stopped at the edge of the Vinegar Hill Cemetery. "I'm sorry. I needed to bring you to see Sheffield's grave. He'd be so happy to finally meet you. I talked about you all the time. Sometimes, he'd ask when you were coming. I was forever saying, "When we see Sugar, she and I'll do such and such."

Sugar put her arm on Lottie's shoulder. "I'm sorry. I wish I'd known him like I did the others."

"He was a special child. I should've known he was not long for this world. He was too kind and sweet for a world such as this. He noticed everything in God's nature. A bird in flight, an ant on the ground, the call of a whippoorwill...all caught his attention. He'd smile from ear to ear and say 'Did you hear that, Mama, or did you see that, Mama?'"

Sugar swallowed the lump in her throat. "Show me where you laid him."

Lottie took Sugar's hand and led her to the site. Right here near this beautiful oak tree. He can listen to the birds all the time. I wanted to bring him back to the mountains before we moved here. He'd have loved where we grew up. I would've had a hard time keeping him inside."

Sugar looked across the hundreds of grave markers. Many had only a creek rock for a headstone. Some were beautiful formed markers with nice sayings. She bit her lip hard.

Lottie continued to talk. "Oh, I know he's not really here, but it gives me peace that he's out in nature that he loved so much."

"I don't think I have ever seen a fuller cemetery in my life. Is it the only one in Clifton?"

"No, there are some at the churches in the area, and all have a right smart amount of graves. Sickness seems to take out a lot of people here. I don't know why, unless it's because we live so close to one another."

Sugar looked into Lottie's eyes. "Somebody, some on of the family, should've been here with you when you buried him. I'm sorry."

"We're a long way from Jackson County. We didn't have money for a telegram and, even if we did, Beck said you wouldn't have time to get here before we had to put him in the ground."

"Did you see his death coming beforehand?"

Lottie wrinkled her forehead. "What do you mean?"

"You and I both know you see things, my sighted sister. Did you know it was coming?"

Lottie folded her arms. "There wasn't a thing I could have done to stop it. Not one thing."

"Of course not. I know that. I didn't mean..."

"Yes, I was warned. There'll be more deaths, too. I knew it the minute I saw the house. It was in my dreams. But, I don't want to talk about it. If there's one thing I can tell you, it's that knowing something don't mean you can stop it. Whatever tells me these things, it doesn't let me know what to do about it, or not that I can tell. I wish Mama was here. Maybe she'd know. Having the second sight is a curse that I hope none of my children get."

"Does it appear that they see things like you do?"

"I try not to talk about it in front of them. They may or may not. They haven't told me anything before it happened, yet."

Sugar said, "I remember the first time you saw something. You told me and Mama that a woman at the church was going to make a chocolate pie for the community dinner. She did. She said it was the first one she'd ever made and, for some reason, she had a hankering to make one THAT day."

Lottie laughed. "I'm glad you reminded me. I didn't remember."

"You were ten years old. It started early."

"It seems to me that the only things I've ever seen are bad. Except maybe for the pie you reminded me about. Why can't I see good things sometimes? I don't want to know about the bad ones. I grieve longer than I would have had I not known."

They walked arm in arm to the house.

***

The following Tuesday morning, the heat was near unbearable. Lottie unbuttoned the upper portion of her dress and held it open. The wind was not quite enough to cool her so she lowered her chin and blew on her breasts. "It's as hot as blue blazes today. I hope this is the last hot day of summer. It's September and should be cooling off some. Whew."

She pulled a handkerchief out of the tie belt at her waist and rubbed the sweat that ran down her neck and slid between her breasts. "I don't rightly know how I would've made it without your help, Sister. This is the last bushel of late season corn. It took us longer to shuck and silk it than it did to cut if off. This hot day makes me want to be in the mountains where the air is cool and fresh. I think I have enough food put up for the winter."

Sugar picked up a corn shuck and filled it with water like it was a bowl. She raised her head, tipped it to the side, and let the water trickle out of the leaf and onto her face. It slid down her neck and soaked the top of her dress. "The wind sure does feel good on a wet dress. Here, let me show you." She cupped her hands and threw water at Lottie. It became a game like what they would've done when they were young girls.

Their laughter was so loud they didn't hear the man walk up until he spoke. "Excuse me, ladies."

Lottie grabbed at the buttons at the top of her dress. Sugar folded her arms across her wet chest.

"I'd like to say a few words to your sister, Miss Lottie. It won't take long." He turned to Sugar and motioned for her to come out to where he stood near the road.

"What needs to be said can be spoken in front of my sister. We don't have secrets from each other."

Red rushed up from under the neck of his shirt and into his face. "Very well then."

He turned his head and stared at Sugar. "I know I don't have much to offer, but I sure need a good woman to be a mother to my three children."

Sugar stepped backward.

According to Beck, this man had been one of the first to welcome him when he started to attend the church. On Sunday, he had brought him over and introduced him to Sugar and Lottie. The women had nodded and walked away quickly. He was a poor widower with small children, but she hadn't thought to tell her sister the particulars.

The gentleman continued, "I promise you that I'll work hard and make a living. You won't have to work in the mill. I may sometimes need help in the fields, just from time to time, but I will only ask you to do that if an emergency arises. You can come and see Miss Lottie anytime you please. You can see her at the church services. I go regularly, and they come fairly often, maybe more so if you were going to be there. I know it would be hard work to raise children, especially those that ain't your own..."

Lottie felt judged. On Sunday, Lottie had dressed the children and took them to Church. She hadn't attended in quite a while, in spite of Beck finding a new church, but she wanted Sugar to be able to tell her parents that the family had attended together. It was terribly hard to attend each Sunday. Her poor babies were pulled out of bed early every day. They needed one day to rest. Even when they didn't make it to the house of the Lord, they still read scripture and prayed.

Sugar reached both arms out and her hands waved from side to side as she tried to silence him. "You stop right there. While I do appreciate a nice..." She coughed. "A nice proposal, such as it is. I can't marry you. I have a family of my own. Two children."

Lottie moaned. Sugar glanced her way with a warning look. "My children and all yours would be too much to ask a man such as yourself to support. Again, I appreciate the proposal, but the answer is no."

Spotty dark red blotches covered his neck and face. "I'm truly sorry. I didn't know you were married and had children. I thought Beck said..."

"Married? Who said anything about being married? I only said I had two children."

Lottie looked from one to the other. If she wasn't so confused herself, she could've laughed at the man standing before them. His mouth was opening and closing, but he didn't make a single sound. He began to rock back and forth until he got up enough motion to turn and run.

Lottie put her hands on her hips and turned to Sugar. "I guess you know I can never darken the door of that church house again."

"Find you another one. There's one on every corner in this town." Sugar went to the steps and sat down. She looked over her shoulder toward the window of the family that lived in the other side of the house. The curtain was slightly open and you could see one eye and a nose sticking between them.

"I guess you may have to move too, Lottie, as your neighbors knows all our dirty laundry as well."

The curtain jerked together so hard the string that held the material broke. The woman ran away from the window. Sugar laughed out loud. Lottie wanted to, but grabbed Sugar's hand and pulled her up. "Let's take a walk up the road and find some trees to shade ourselves. We need to talk."

When they were out of earshot of the houses, Lottie stopped. She took a deep breath. "Why would you lie like that? You could've turned that man down without making him think all of us are trash."

Sugar bit her lower lip for a bit, then pulled her upper lip between her teeth. Lottie tapped her toe.

"I wasn't lying. I do have two children. They're with Mama."

Tears came into Lottie's eyes. "You have two children and you never told me? Mama never told me in any of her letters. What's wrong with you all? Why would you keep such a thing from me? And you ain't married? Whose babies are they? What man have you been keeping company with?"

Sugar held out her hands. "That's way too many questions to remember and still answer them. Let's sit down on this tree root, and I'll try to explain.

"First of all, Mama didn't tell you because I asked her not to. You'd have tried to come home. With the first baby, it was too dangerous for you to come back because Owen was alive, even if any of us had the money. By the time the second came along,

I guess I was too embarrassed. They're two and almost one year old, one boy and one girl. As to what man they belong to, that's another story that I don't want to talk about on this trip, if I ever do. There'll not be no bastardy bonds put on the records in the courts of Jackson County for my children. You need to understand that I don't ever plan on marrying. I don't need a man to raise a child...or two. It's not something I aimed to happen. Second, I ain't trash like you suggested. I know it's an embarrassment to Papa and Mama, and I've moved out of the house. Not too far away, but close enough that I can check on them. I take in washing and do ironing for people. I've cleaned a few houses and did some cooking. I grow a garden and put up all the food I can. It's still a hard life, but I'm doing ok. When Mama offered to keep the children and let me come and see you, I was happy as a tick on a hound dog. We were always closer than the others. Mama wanted to come, but she wasn't able. She's been sick a lot this last year. Worrying about you and me don't help none, I'm sure. She thought it best that I did the traveling."

Lottie wiped her tears with her dress tail. "I hate I'm not there helping to tend to Papa and Mama. I was always worried Papa was going to die. He was so sick the year before I left. But he pulled out of that one. Now, Mama's not well. It ain't fair, Sugar. I want to come home."

Sugar reached down and took Lottie's hand. "Life ain't never been fair. Not for anybody, but it seems like it's harder on our family than most. You do what you have to do, just like me. So as you know, Papa ain't completely well. He talks about how his heart feels heavy at the thought of being old and his time passing away so quickly. He just knows he'll never be remembered, and that he'll fade from our memories. Not quickly of course, but he's afraid his face and the way he taught us will become dimmer day by day until it fades from the view of everyone that knew him. He thinks we won't tell our children and our children's children about him. He talks in such a way that makes me not want to go and see him. He thinks our family has a spell on it from all the mean things from the past. He's sure if he's not here, we'll all go to the dogs."

Lottie took a heavy breath. "We won't forget him. My older children will remember, but some of my brood has never seen his face. It makes me cry to think about that." She dabbed at her eyes with the handkerchief she pulled from her bosom. "I'm homesick. For you. For Mama and Papa. For the mountains. I want the life I had...but without Owen."

Sugar hugged her sister. "I believe that Beck will take care of you as best he can. You go wherever he thinks you should. Worrying about Owen and how he died and by who's hand is not worth your time. As for Beck killing that hateful first husband of yours, only he knows if he did or not. If he didn't, only the one that did it knows for sure. The people I know say that Owen more than likely died a natural death. They said he was as yellow as a sunflower, so it sounds like to me he'd been sick for some time. He always was a drinker. That might have killed him. Even if Beck did, it was for a good reason. You never know, I might've been the one that killed him, feeding him a little poison here and there."

"I don't believe that. I can't see you feeding him anything. Both of you hated to be in the same room together. For the most part, you have a true feeling of right and wrong, and you wouldn't have killed him."

Sugar smiled and slipped her arm around Lottie. "Knowing right and wrong is the very thing that could have made me do it. He's run you down to anybody that will listen, when all the time he's the one that's been mean and low-down. There are two sides to every story. I knew both of them. He deserved to die. The people he gossiped to about you only heard one side. I wish they could've heard the other story. Not long ago, our preacher preached a sermon about this very thing. He gave a scripture out of Proverbs. I think it was Proverbs 18. It said something akin to a person that speaks first about a matter, it seems he's right, until someone comes along and disputes it. Somebody needed to disagree with what Owen said. But nobody would. So it was best to just shut him up."

Lottie and Sugar circled down River Road and sat on a sand bank, away from houses and people.

Lottie was so quiet that Sugar asked, "What's ailing you now?"

"I need to know what happened with Owen. Everything. From the beginning."

"My goodness, Lottie. Are you not satisfied that he won't hurt you or anyone else again? I told you leave it alone."

Lottie heard a strange sound in Sugar's voice. "What do you mean 'or someone else'? Who else would he hurt?"

"All right, I'll tell you something. Make yourself comfortable and do not, I say DO NOT, interrupt me."

Lottie nodded.

"I worked in town for a woman, doing washing and cleaning her house, for a few dollars a month and any extra food she had leftover I would take for my children."

Lottie started to speak.

"Not a word, I told you. This ain't about me, but that's why I was working for the woman."

Lottie squeezed her lips together to let Sugar know she would be quiet.

"She had a daughter that had been widowed. She had moved home from Asheville to be with family. Owen took a liking to her. They seemed as thick as thieves. Things were moving toward a wedding. I tried to stay out of their way, but Owen knew I worked there. One day he came to their house while the woman and her daughter were away visiting. He knew they were gone, but he came a day he knew I was there."

Sugar laughed at Lottie's wide eyes.

"No I didn't murder him right then and there. I did want to, though. You know there's no love lost between him and me. His eyes were blood red, and I knew he'd been drinking. We argued over you. We were both yelling and screaming when the woman and her daughter came home. They were angry at me for acting mean toward him until they realized he'd been drinking. They threw him out."

"I bet he was mad at you," Lottie snapped. "I want you to tell me who you think killed him."

"Just be glad he's six foot under."

Lottie shook her head. "You're scaring me. You killed him, didn't you?"

"Just rest assured that there were lots of people that wanted him dead. Yes, I could've killed him. So could've Beck. Maybe even others, I'm sure. But I still think it might have been all his drinking that did it. Maybe even a bad batch of 'shine. Leave it as a mystery that nobody knows for sure."

"You're not going to tell me everything you know, are you?" Lottie narrowed her eyes.

Sugar laughed. "Probably not. Again, be happy he's gone and will never again hurt another woman. Let's talk about something else. I only have two more days, and I have to go home."

Chapter 16

January 1902

"What's wrong with you all? Somebody say something. This table is too quiet." Lottie looked from one to the other.

They poked at their food, and all ate without saying a word.

"Got a lot on our mind, I suspect," Beck offered.

Lottie laid down her fork. "What is so strong on your mind Beck Radford that you can't talk to this family?"

"I've been studying about a man from the mill. He worked on the loom. He pulled a handle two months ago, and the lever slipped because the gear was too tight. He mashed his thumb. It's on his right hand, and now it's infected. He can't use his hand at all. His whole hand is swelled tighter than a tick. He's been out of work for these two months and hasn't had a cent to live on since. The company let him have one month rent-free at the house, but now they've told him that his family and him have to get out. There's another worker coming, and they'll need the house for that family. I can't help but wonder what would happen to you and the children if that was me. It just don't seem right. It happened because they didn't work on the loom. He reported a problem several weeks ago, and yet they're not taking care of him. If somebody got hurt on my farm, I'd take responsibility for him. It's only right. They don't show that they care."

Brody said, "His son is the same age as me, but he works as a runner in the cloth room. He's the only other person in the family that worked. They can't live off his pay alone."

Lottie stood and took her plate to the dishpan. "What will they do?"

"I talked to him today, and he says they plan on trying to get enough money to move up to North Carolina near his brother. He's really sick. The hand has turned black."

Lottie's breast heaved in a sigh. "It's always something here. Accidents, fevers, death, always trouble on every side."

***

Florence grabbed the sheet with both hands, sat up, and yelled "Get the doctor, Fate. Get him quick. This baby is a-coming tonight." She fell back on the bed.

Fate kicked the covers back. He put his feet in the legs of his britches and stuck his feet in his boots. "I'll get him now. Will you be ok until I get back?"

"Run up and get Lottie to come down here. It will be a little while before she has to fix breakfast for her family. Maybe you can get back with the doctor before she has to leave. I don't want to be alone."

Fate pulled the suspenders over his shoulders and grabbed his hat.

Florence motioned for Fate to come close to the bed. "I want to ask you to do something for me. It'll seem strange, but do exactly what I say." She moaned and pulled herself up again using the covers to help her rise.

When the pain eased, she continued, "The usual way for you to come back to the house after fetching the doctor would be across the bridge at Dexter Mill. I want you to go up the river and cross at Mill Number One. Use that route to come here."

"I don't need to do that. That way will take too long." Fate sat down on Florence's side of the bed. "You might have that baby while I'm gone. He lives behind the Rock Store, and that would be the long way around, and I..."

"I know it's the long way, but please promise me you'll do it. I have a reason, and I'll tell you about it someday. For now, just please do as I ask without any question. Promise me!" Florence began to cry.

Fate stared at her. "I will, but I don't like it. I'll send Lottie down here and go get the doctor."

"Thank you, Fate. Thank you for doing what I ask."

***

Lottie didn't knock. "The baby's coming, Fate says."

"Yes. It'll be born tonight. Let's hope the doctor gets here in time."

"Did you do like we planned? Which direction did you tell Fate to come back with the doctor?"

Florence smiled. "Exactly like we talked about. He'll bring the doctor back by way of Mill Number One. I have to say I'm a little worried. There's a railroad track there, too. What if it's supposed to happen there instead of Dexter Mill?"

Lottie looked at the tears in Florence's eyes. She sat down beside her. "It's all we can do. If it's meant to be, there's nothing we can do to stop it, but we had to try. Either way, we know we did the best we could."

"Wouldn't it have been better to tell him the dream? He could've been careful down at Dexter Bridge."

Lottie twisted her fingers. "He wouldn't have believed me, I fear. Most people don't. In fact, it seems that most try to show me that it won't happen like I say it's going to. I still believe it was best not to give him the particulars. I felt that changing the way and place things happened in the whole dream was safer."

Lottie built a fire in the stove and started water to boil. She tore sheets into strips from material that Florence had bought for the birth.

They made small talk for a while until the pangs of childbirth made conversation hard. In the distance, they heard the whistle of the train. Lottie sat down and held Florence's hand, and they stared at each other.

In a few minutes, Fate shoved the door open and held it for the doctor.

Florence broke into tears.

"I hurried. That long way around took more time. Are you faring well?"

She laughed through her tears. "I'm fine. You got him here in plenty of time."

This time she screamed with pain. The doctor barked out orders. The birth came quickly for a first child.

Lottie slipped out the door and left the family to coo over their baby.

***

Lottie hurried the family off to work. She wanted to get back to Florence as quickly as she could.

She cracked the door and peeked in. Florence was sitting up in bed, and the baby was at her breast.

"How is Mama and baby boy doing?" She asked.

"Me and little Fate are just fine and dandy."

Lottie clapped her hands. “You named him after his Papa.”

Florence laid Little Fate on the bed and looked at Lottie. “You’re not going to believe this. It’s a wonderful story.”

“Not much surprises me, and I believe about everything I hear.” She laughed.

“Well, when you left last night, Fate told me about his trip coming back with the doctor. He said, just before they got to Mill Number One, the train came by. They had to sit there and wait for that dang train. He was madder than a hornet.”

Lottie laughed. She grabbed Florence and hugged her. “We stopped it. That was a reason that I saw it all.” Lottie started to cry. “I’ve always been terribly mad when I see these things or dream the dreams. It’s like it was hopeless. I always wanted to know why I saw it if I couldn’t do anything about it. Perhaps it was to teach me that the dreams are genuine. The signs could actually stop some bad things from happening.”

Florence pulled Lottie’s hands into her own. “Thank you for telling me. It saved my husband’s life. My baby’s Papa. You’re the best friend a woman could have.”

***

Beck took off his hat and stepped into Polly’s house. This was only the second time he’d been inside. Before, he never took the time to look around. It was a large structure, perfect for a boarding house.

Peter pulled out a chair. "Papa, sit here at the table. I'll get you a drink of water. Billy and Sarah are upstairs. I'll fetch 'em. It should be less than half an hour before Maude gets here. They want us to go to town as a family. I knew you'd want to if it meant we'd be together, so I accepted for you. I'll be back in a minute."

Beck twirled his hat in his hands. Peter handed him the water and left to get the others.

"Hello, Beck."

He jumped and looked around. "Hello, Polly. I'm sorry to intrude, but Peter wanted me to sit and wait for the others. We're going out for a while."

"I know. It's a good thing that you've come to see the children like you have. I have to say I'm surprised, but glad."

Beck's face turned red. "It shocks me that you approve our visits. I don't know what happened to us, Polly. All I tried to do was make a living for this family. I came home every chance I could."

"Did you really? It didn't seem like it. You were hardly ever there. It was hard without your help."

Beck bowed his head and said, "I'm truly sorry for hurting you or them. There's nothing I can do to change it now, even though I'd like to."

Polly said, "It's all water under the bridge. You have another family. I own a boarding house and I'm trying to make a living. We each have our own life."

He nodded. “Peter is helping you with money he said. He’s a good boy.”

“They’re all good children.”

Beck twisted his hat in circles and avoided looking at her.

Polly stood up and re-arranged pictures on a nearby table. “In November of 1900, my cousin, the one that’s the sheriff in Jackson County North Carolina, he wrote me a letter and asked some questions about you.”

The table shook when Beck jumped up. “He did? What did he want?”

“The questions were about you and a man named Owen Thompson. He wanted to know if I thought you were capable of doing harm to another person, someone like your wife’s first husband.”

Beck raised his eyebrows. “What did you say? What do you think?”

“I wrote him back and told him I didn’t think you could harm another living thing. You might not have been the best husband or father, but you were not a mean person.”

“Thank you for that. Did they say anything else?”

Polly looked Beck in the eye. “They said you were in the area when her husband died, and there was some gossip that you wanted him dead so you could marry his wife. You wouldn’t do anything like that, would you?”

Beck sat back down. “I thought you felt I couldn’t hurt another living thing?”

Polly sat down across the table from Beck. "I do feel that way. You might not be the best husband, but you were never mean to me or the children. But I need you to tell me that you didn't do it."

They heard the others run down the steps. Peter ran into the room. He stopped when he saw his Papa and Mama sitting at the table together.

Beck stood up. "Are you ready to go?"

"The others will be right down." Peter looked out the window. "Here comes Maude, so we're ready."

Beck drained the last of the water from the glass and set it on the table. "Good to see you again, Polly. The children will be back in a couple of hours." He tipped his hat and left.

Chapter 17

June 1902

Annie May and Lizzie walked side by side to the river.

Lizzie pulled Annie May's hand and tried to make her go faster. "I love Sunday's. The picnics and fun we have. Sometimes I think I live for Sundays."

They stopped at the bottom of the hill and caught their breath. They stood shoulder to shoulder and looked about for friends to sit with. Annie May shivered in the hot sun.

"What are you shaking about?" Lizzie asked.

Annie May shrugged her shoulders. "I don't know. Just a chill went up my spine. I guess somebody walked over my future grave."

"What?" Lizzie laughed.

"Mama says when you shake like that, or have that feeling, that someone just walked over where your grave will be."

Lizzie put her hands on her hips and laughed. "Sakes alive! You don't really believe that stuff do you?"

Annie bit her lip. "Uh. Maybe not. I guess I thought it was true because my mama told me. Where I come from, everybody says it. Now that I think about it, it does seem odd." She changed the subject. "I'm so glad you're my friend here in Clifton. Well, you're actually the only close friend I've ever had."

Lizzie raised her eyebrows. "You didn't have friends in the mountains?"

"I guess my brothers and sisters were my friends. I had cousins that came to play, but my Papa didn't like people coming to our house. He didn't want us going to Grandpa's and Grandma's either, but Mama slipped us over to see them sometimes."

Lizzie looked amazed. She stood next to Annie by the tree. "Your Papa don't seem like that kind of man to me. He never minds when I come over."

"It wasn't this Papa. It was my other Papa." Lottie continued toward the river.

Lizzie grabbed Annie and pulled her around. "You have two Papas?"

"No, we used to have one Papa, and now we have another one. My real papa was named Owen Thompson."

"Did your first Papa pass away?"

"Yes, he died after Mama moved us to Tennessee with Beck." Annie May bit her lip. "Please don't tell nobody else. Promise me. I shouldn't have told you. Mama would be mad."

"I won't tell." Lizzie promised.

***

Lottie took the arm offered to her by Beck. She picked up the basket of food she had packed for them.

"I feel like a princess escorted on your arm to the river side. It's like we're going to a ball. We'll dance in the garden until its dark." Lottie smiled.

"I don't dance much, you know that. I have two left feet. The sand on the river shoal is not much of a garden either." Beck grinned at Lottie.

"You don't play music. You don't dance. What made me think you were husband material?"

August grabbed Lottie's arm. "Do I have to watch Tolliver all afternoon? Can't I stay up here on the bank? I don't want to go near the water."

"Of course you can't stay up here. Tolliver will take a nap on the quilt beside me later, and you can play with the others. It looks like everyone your age is down by the water. If you want to play with them, that's where you'll have to go."

"I don't want to play with them. I want to sit up here and watch."

Lottie set her basket down and bent to look August in the eyes. "What are you talking about?

You love the water. Look, they're wading and catching crawdads. You can splash and have a good time."

"Please don't make me go down there." August started to cry.

"What's wrong? Tell me why you are acting like this."

August looked from Beck to Lottie and took a deep breath. "I had a dream last week. People were in the water everywhere but not swimming. They were screaming and yelling for help. They were hanging in trees and floating by as they sat on houses or hung onto logs. What if we're down there and that happens?"

Lottie's voice was shaky. "There's not enough water being held back by the dam to take down houses and trees if the dam broke. It was just a dream."

"There was a woman on top of a house with her little bitty baby, and they were screaming. The house floated by me, spinning in the water. I knew they were going to die."

Lottie leaned close to her and asked, "It wasn't any of our family was it? Was it anyone you know?"

"I didn't see anybody I knew, but that woman on the house looked like someone I've met before."

Lottie pulled August into her arms. "It was a dream, baby girl."

"You have dreams, and they come true. What if my dream comes true? I didn't tell it for a week. You say never do that. That's right, ain't it?"

Lottie looked at Beck, begging for help.

Beck pulled Lottie up and bent down by August. “You can sit up here on the bank for the time being. Come on down if you change your mind. Right now, your Mama wants to have a few minutes of good time. I’ll get Annie May to watch Tolliver after he wakes up from his nap”

Beck picked up the basket from beside Lottie. “I guess that brought you back to our real life. No time for balls and dancing.”

Lottie’s smile didn’t reach her eyes.

“I wouldn’t trade this life for the other anyways.”

Lottie prayed from deep within her heart. *Please don’t let her have the gift, God.*

***

Two boys on the lower sand played Mumbley Peg. They faced one another. Each spread their feet about shoulder’s length apart. One boy took an open pocket knife and threw it to stick in the ground as close as possible to his own foot. The other boy did the same.

Lizzie and Annie May watched them for a bit then moved closer to the older boys near the dam.

“Oooee. The saps arising in the young men today.” Lizzie pushed her elbow into Annie May’s side. “That boy over there is looking at you real quare like. I think he likes you.”

"What boy?" Annie May looked at one of the boys flipping a coin into the air and slapping it on his other hand.

"Not there. Over there." She pointed to a group of young men sitting on the hillside. "He pointed our way once."

"Them ain't boys! They're men! Besides, it was probably you they're looking at. You're the pretty one."

"That's silly. You're prettier than me." Lizzie said truthfully.

"It don't matter. They're too old for either one of us. As usual though, you're looking for an older man."

Lizzie wrinkled her nose. "We had these same words last year not long after you came to work. My Mama married at fourteen. That's just two years older than you. If you're going to marry at fourteen, you'd better be looking now so you can find a good one. A handsome man for sure."

Annie May shoved Lizzie. "I don't mind him being handsome, but I want one that has some money like you suggested, or at least one that'll work and make money. I want to move back to the mountains."

The look on Lizzie's face made Annie realize how unkind her words had sounded. "I'd have enough money to build you a house right next to mine, and you and your handsome husband and pretty babies would move in right beside me."

They laughed so hard, they fell down on the ground. The young men made their way down to where the girls sat.

***

If August hadn't dampened Lottie's spirits, seeing everyone in their fine clothes would have. It wasn't that her dress was so bad, but it was that the others were so good, fine frills and lace. Theirs looked new. Her clothes looked old and faded.

"It's about time you got here, slow poke." Florence jabbed Lottie in the side. "Bring your quilt over here in the shade beside mine and Fate's. We'll send the men away when they start playing music. Maybe they'll teach Beck a thing or two. I can help you watch your children seeing mine will sleep the whole time. He's a good baby."

Lottie clapped her hands and laughed. "One of these days you're going to have a dozen running around."

Florence smiled. "Oh my! A dozen. I hope not. And to think I was worried. What a waste of time that was. I should've known. I've never known anyone in my family that didn't have a litter amount of babies."

Lottie hugged Florence. "You've only been married two years. Mine and Owen's first baby, Brody, came along not long after we married."

Others nearby began to whisper. Florence frowned at Lottie. "You best keep your voice down.

You've already learned this town is full of gossips. It'll be all over town by sundown. I can hear their voices now. 'She had to get married to some man named Owen, and that man with her is named Beck. You put two and two together'. Can't you hear them?"

"They'd be adding the wrong numbers." Lottie whispered to Florence as she spread her quilt and set down her basket on the edge to keep the wind from blowing it away. She laid Tolliver on the corner and patted him until he fell back to sleep. "Owen is dead and gone, and I've every right to be married to Beck."

"Do you really think that matters to those old biddies? The truth is not juicy enough. They'd rather make up what they want to hear, and what sounds better, so the others will listen.

Lottie sighed. "Anyway, don't worry about them. Let's listen to the men playing tunes. I don't count on Beck learning anything about music, but maybe you can teach him to dance."

Chapter 18

November 1902

Lottie looked at the small, empty hole in the ground. She raised her eyes to the hand-full of people on either side of the grave. They stood far apart from one another. Both women and men covered their mouths and noses with handkerchiefs. No one spoke to the other. She didn't know a single person in attendance. She'd come because of Beck and the thought of no kin left to mourn the child.

Beck shuffled to one end of the grave and another man to the other end. They lowered the casket into the ground. The two men had made the simple pine chest earlier that day.

This was the fifth grave to complete a circle around a large grave, each one fresh. They lay out like rays of light from the sun. The group of graves was unadorned except for a plain headstone made from creek rock.

The Black Death had swept away the entire family. A baby of one year was the first to pass away. A day later, two others had perished, a boy ten and, later that afternoon, a girl of three. One day later, the oldest son had perished. The next day it had taken both parents. Today they buried the last of the family, a girl of eight years.

The preacher had gone from house to house in the early morning to ask someone to meet him at the company store if they were willing to build a casket. Beck and the other man were the only two to show up.

Lottie compared the dreadful disease that had crept into the village to that of the death angel in Egypt that she had read about in the Bible. Only this time, it didn't take only the first born but entire families.

The men threw dirt into the hole and onto the box. Lottie stared into the trees beyond the cemetery and thought about a lady she had met on the trolley. She spoke of how the fever came like a whirlwind and carried the awful disease through Clifton and Spartanburg. It all began with one family and a visit from outsiders.

A month before, on a hill above Mill Number One, the people were awakened by screams from the home of the Burgin family. Clyde, the six year old son of Virgil and Coosey Burgin had died.

Coosey's sister had died of complications of childbirth ten days before, and mourners had come by train from as far away as Asheville and Atlanta. They did more than pay their respects when they came. They brought in the most dreaded disease Lottie had ever seen. It started with a sore throat and fever. It hurt to turn their head, and there were knots all down the side of their neck. The Strangler had come to Spartanburg County.

Everyone walked with their head down...on the street, in the store, at church. Beck said that at the mill you would hear people cry and see people gather around someone and comfort them as death after death affected another family.

Beck and Lottie tried to get the children to go out and play with friends, but they refused. She knew they were afraid. The school was closed.

Lottie went to the store one day and grew lightheaded. She had to sit down on the ground to keep from fainting. She realized that she had been holding her breath, afraid to breathe. At the store, she turned away from anyone that came near her. *Don't breathe on me. Please don't even look at me.* She was afraid to talk to anyone. She even turned and headed the other way when she saw Florence coming toward her. Any person could deliver your death sentence.

There were rumors that the store might close. Not once had she heard that the mill might close though.

So many people were dying that they could hardly be counted. The storekeeper kept a list on the front door with the names of those that had passed. Every day, someone would come and add one, two, or even three names at a time. You never knew who would be next on the list. You worried that a member of your family might appear there before it all ended.

***

Near dawn, Tolliver began to shake and cry and his body was dry and feverish. He took a few small pulls at her breast, drew back, and cried a most pitiful cry. A small stream of milk ran out the corner of his mouth onto her chest.

Beck pulled on his trousers and ran to fetch the doctor.

He returned without him. “He’s at a house on the hill beside Mill One. He’s been there all night. All have the same sickness.”

Lottie dabbed her eyes and rocked Tolliver. She sat in a straight chair and snapped her back against the back slats of the chair as she rocked. It bounced the small bundle in her arms, and he would stop crying for a moment.

“Get me that cod liver oil. I’ll try a dose of that.”

Beck brought it and a spoon to Lottie.

Tolliver’s cry and cough were dry and hacking. He gagged, and Lottie could see a black-looking wad that looked like a net in the back of his throat.

Beck stood over her shoulder. "The doctor's wife asked if the rest of us wanted to take a thing called an annie-toxin. I told her I didn't know, but I'd try to get back to her."

Lottie shook her head. "I heard people talk about that down at the store. Out in Saint Louie, there were thirteen children that died from taking it. I heard a man read about it in the Spartanburg Journal. Another person said that in the same paper it told about three families that were saved by the annie-toxin. I don't know what to believe. What do you think?"

"I'm scared. I don't know what to do." Beck bit his lip.

Lottie patted her foot and looked toward the door where the other children lay on their bed. She pointed at the door. "I think you should get back there and get the annie-toxin. I can't stand to watch our family die and not try to do all we can."

Beck ran out of the house and down the hill.

***

"Where's the annie-toxin?" Lottie paced the floor with Tolliver in her arms.

Beck shook his head. "The doctor took the last dose to somebody else. He's coming here next to check Tolliver. He feels sure it's diphtheria. It'll be a week before they get any more of that medicine."

"Why didn't you get it the first time you were there?" Lottie gritted her teeth.

"I didn't know what to do. You didn't know at first either. Don't blame me." Beck folded his arms. "Why didn't you dream about this and tell us it was coming? You're the sighted sister! Why can't you dream something about our family that can help?"

Lottie's eyes stared hard and straight at him. "I'm going to make believe you never said that. You think I wouldn't do that if I could? I don't pick and choose what comes to me, as much as I'd like to."

Beck reached out to his son's head and rubbed back his dark fuzz. "He's not doing good. If the doctor don't come..."

Lottie asked, "If he does come, then what? You and I both have been around this disease for over a week. So have the children. There's no getting away from it in this crowded place. There's death on every hand. You built a coffin last week and two this week. There are too many new graves in the cemetery to count the number without looking at them. There's no one going to Pest Row. That filled up weeks ago."

Beck snapped. "Pest row is full every day, but new people come in to take the place of those who died the day before."

Lottie sat down and pulled Tolliver close.

Beck poured a cup of coffee. "You stop blood. Your mama taught you to take off warts. Why didn't she teach you something really useful like how to stop a baby from dying?"

Lottie watched her baby boy's breaths grow further and further apart.

Beck choked. “If you’d used your gifts to know this, we could’ve left here in time.”

Lottie stood up and handed Tolliver to Beck. “I did tell you. It was the day we moved in. I said ‘There’s death in this house’. You know the dream I had about us living here. Three coffins…one at a time. This is number two. I wonder who’ll be number three. Why didn’t you believe me then?” She grabbed an iron skillet and slung it on the stove. They had to eat before they left for work. You might have a baby that’s dying, but the others still had to eat if they were going to work. Lottie cried as she laid fat-back into the skillet.

***

The dishes could wait. She didn’t care if they ever got washed. She scooped up her baby from the bed and carried him near the stove for heat. He was shaking.

Breathing came harder and harder for Tolliver. Later, his coughing had almost stopped. His eyes were slightly open, he gasped for breath, and a death rattle shook in his chest.

Lottie sat with slouched shoulders. She pulled Tolliver to her breast and held him with a tight grip. She pulled out a breast and pulled his lips near the nipple. He didn’t open his mouth, but she held him like that and watched the last breaths leave his body.

She looked up at the ceiling, and tears filled her eyes. In the distance, there were cries of others in the same difficulty as her. They had to sit alone with their sick family as the others worked in the mills. Each new wail meant another mother had watched her baby die.

Lottie laid Tolliver on the bed and went to the door. She watched Annie May, Brody, and August climb the hill from the mill toward the house. Beck was a few yards behind them. He walked with his head down.

She stepped out on the porch. They looked at her without saying a word. She reached in her apron pocket and pulled out money she had gotten from the jar in the chicken house. She pushed it at Beck.

"Go and buy lumber to build your son a coffin."

Beck fell to his knees and screamed. "Noooooo. Oh God, no." He shook his fist toward the sky.

He cried more with this death than the others, just like in the dream. This was *his* son. "Get your fist down. Don't go blaming Him. It ain't God's fault. It don't do any good, and we've got three others to think about. We need to get Tolliver in the ground then scrub down this house."

Lottie walked in the house, and her eyes fell on the calendar. November 20, 1902. A date she'd never forget.

Beck turned and motioned for Brody to follow him. He'd need help, but everyone else had their own sorrows with which to contend.

***

There were very few people in the store when Beck and Brody came in. Two men stood beside the bin with casket handles and hinges. Beck walked back outside and found several smooth boards and brought them inside to the counter. By now, the others had moved on, and Beck reached out and picked up a hinge. He laid it back down and picked up a smaller one.

Brody said, “Were those men buying hardware for caskets, too? If everybody comes here, there won’t be enough hinges and handles at this store to take care of all the dead.”

The storekeeper came to their side. “I have a supply coming in by wagon this afternoon from Spartanburg. That might have some others to choose from.”

Beck picked up another small one that matched the one in his hand. “These will do. I need to get the box made for my son as soon as possible.” Beck looked up. “I won’t need the handles to match. He was only a baby, and I can carry him in my arms.”

The storekeeper reached out his hand. “Let me help you with that. I’m sorry about your baby. The sickness is taking people right and left.”

Beck nodded. “Death of a family member is never easy, but a child is the hardest of all. It’s hard to pick up the pieces and move on.”

Brody picked up a piece of sandpaper and showed Beck. He nodded. “I want to make it the nicest I’ve ever made.” He picked around in another holder and found corner pieces for decoration.

Beck went to a small table stacked with baby blankets. When he felt a soft woolen blanket, he brought it to the counter and laid it with his other purchases.

"There'll be no charge for the hinges. The mill owners said if anyone made their own caskets that I was not to charge for the boards or metal fasteners. The corner pieces, sandpaper, and blanket will be all you have to buy."

"I thank you and the owners." Beck said as tears gathered in his eyes.

***

They carried the supplies to the back of the house. Beck pulled out a saw, hammer, and nails.

Beck laid his arm outward along the board as he measured how Tolliver had fit along the inside of his arm when he had held him. He allowed two inches at top and bottom, and, with a nail, he scratched the length on the plank.

The hammer fell, and so did the tears. He spread the blanket inside and tacked it to the edges.

Beck pounded in the last nail on the hinge. He picked up four nails and the hammer and went inside to get his son.

***

As soon as the burial was over, Lottie ran home and jerked the covers off the bed. She rushed outside and threw them in the pot of boiling water that Beck had started in the back yard. A knife lay on the ground beside a cake of lye soap. She picked up both and scraped half the slab into the water.

Inside the house, she jerked the slip off Tolliver's pillow. Her hand held the end where his head had laid, and she felt a lump. She pulled the string that held the end of the pillow seam and broke it. Feathers fell to the floor. A wad of light colored feathers and one small dark one fell out with the loose goose down.

Lottie gasped and sat down in the floor. She scraped her hands across the loose feathers until she found the small gob of dark feathers woven together, the color of Tolliver's hair, like a tiny cap. It was a Death Crown.

"A sign from God," she said aloud. Not that she had any doubt that babies went straight into the arms of God, but to find a feather crown gave her sweet peace. It was three inches wide and had tiny feathers that swept to the right into a round circle, and felt firm to her touch. She reached up and pulled a small cord that was stuck to the crown. It was attached to the feathers, much like the birth cord the granny woman had cut after he was born. She had laid him on this thin pillow when she cut it.

When she had unpacked the things that Beck had brought with them to Tennessee, when they first moved away from North Carolina, he had one larger one like it in his bag. He told her he'd come up on it in his Mama's pillow after her death.

Beck didn't seem sentimental, but this was one thing that he wouldn't part with.

There was a box, far beneath their bed, that held a few things she wanted to keep. She added this to the box wrapped in a page of a newspaper. Someday she would tell how she found it to the family, but for now it was a sign from God to her, and she didn't want to talk about it.

Chapter 19

March 1903

It was the wettest spring Lottie could remember. She sat on the floor and scrubbed the mud the children and Beck had tromped in for the past two days. Yesterday, she had run in and out the back door to puke. She wished these months of sickness were behind her. No doubt, she was having a boy again. Sickness like this happened every time she carried a boy. The nausea had eased an hour ago, enough time to fix supper and start to mop up the mud in the kitchen. The dirty floors in the rest of the house would have to wait for another day.

There was a continuous knocking on the front door. “I’ll be there in a minute. Hold your tater.” Lottie crawled to a chair and pulled up her aching body.

The woman that stood there was tall and heavy built. The fan in her hand whipped back and forth and stirred barely enough air to blow the hair on her forehead. “Is Beck here? I need to talk to him.” She set down the baby she held in her arms, and placed him between her feet while she talked. He looked a little less than a year old.

“He’s at the mill like the other operatives. He don’t get off until six o’clock.” Lottie held tight to the closed door and watched her through the screen.

The woman tiptoed slightly and looked over Lottie’s head at the inside of the house. “Got quite a fancy little house here, don’t you, what with screen doors and lots of room for a mill house.”

Lottie bit her lip. “The company put on the screens this spring when the fever was so bad. Somebody said it might be mosquitos carrying the sickness. I have to admit I like the door. If you live around here, they’ll put screens on your house. They should’ve told your husband that, if he works at the mill.”

“I live in Spartanburg in my own house. There’s no one to make repairs or add comforts but me.”

Lottie opened the screen and stepped out. “Do I know you?”

The woman didn’t answer, and Lottie asked, “Does Beck know you? I didn’t know he knew anybody in Spartanburg.”

“He knows me quite well. We go back a long ways.” The baby looked up at his Mama and stuck out his lower lip.

Butterflies fluttered in Lottie’s stomach. “Where did you meet? How long have you known each other?”

The woman laughed. "Tennessee. I'm the mother of his children." Lottie's face drained of color. "To at least four of his children, anyway. I take it you're the mother of the rest."

Lottie stepped back and felt for a chair to sit in.

The woman jerked the screen wide open, grabbed up her baby, and stepped inside. "Are you going to faint?"

"I don't think so." Lottie pulled a handkerchief from inside the bosom of her dress. She dabbed at the beads of sweat on her brow. "Have you seen Beck since we've been here?"

"Yep. He comes real often to see his children in Spartanburg. He has for almost two years."

The ringing in her ears got loud, and the last thing she saw was like a black cloud that swooped in and wrapped around her.

***

The hand hit her jaw with a pop. Her jaw stung. The woman slapped one cheek of Lottie's and then the other. "Are you alright?"

"I...I think so." Lottie sat up.

"What happened to you? Are you normally a fainter?" The woman stooped beside her.

"I've never done that before. Everything went black, and the next thing I knew, I was in the floor." Lottie put her hands on her large belly and rubbed.

"You slipped right out of the chair like water running out a cistern pump and into the floor without a sound. I've never seen anything like it."

The woman picked up the lap baby and put a corner of a table chair on his dress tail. She helped Lottie into the chair. Lottie crossed her arms on the table and put her head down.

"My name is Polly. You must be Lottie. Peter says that Beck talks about you. He never says a word to me about the life he's living now."

The room spun circles around her, and Lottie felt liquid burn the back of her throat. She ran to the door and leaned over the side of the porch and vomited.

***

Lottie rolled her body to the wall and covered her face with her hands.

Beck touched her on the back. "I'm sorry I didn't tell you sooner. I didn't think you'd want to know."

Lottie jerked her body away from him. "Why would you think that? You think I'd rather be talked about behind my back by you and everybody else? People must see you meeting another woman in the city. People are probably laughing at me."

She turned back to face Beck. "Why did you hide this from me? I really want to know why you went to see Polly. I understand why you visit your children. But she came here to mock me. She probably figured you never told me you visit her. It makes me mad that she was right!"

Beck looked out the window. "I don't visit *her.* I never found the children. They found me. I told you that."

"Look at me, Beck. Look me in the eye when you lie to me."

"I ain't lying. It's the truth if ever I told it." Beck looked Lottie in the eye and never blinked. "The first time I went to see them at Polly's house was because Peter had a black eye when he met me at the trolley one Sunday. Polly runs a boarding house in the city, and one of the men that lives there hit Peter. To meet at the house made it easier on Peter, and the others agreed only to visit with me if I came there. Polly was hardly ever there, so I went back a few more times.

They stared at one another. Lottie looked away. "I reckon I believe you, but don't hide things from me again. I lived with secrets with Owen, and I ain't doing that no more. I hated it. Your other children needed to see their Papa. I'll be the first to agree on that. But, you should see them somewhere else and not at Polly's. I don't want you there."

"There's nothing else to say. I'd still try to see my children no matter what anyone says. I will go anywhere I have to go to see them."

Lottie didn't know what to say. He had not been as pigheaded about anything like this since she had met him.

Beck smiled. “Oh, how they’ve grown. One by one, the others finally let me talk with them when I started to come to the house. Now, it’s almost like I never left. The first few times, they would not call me anything. They’d say ‘hey you’, but now they call me Papa again. The only reason I went to Polly’s and the only reason I would do it again is to protect any one of them. I swear.”

Lottie sat up on the side of the bed. She looked at Beck out of the corner of her eye. His hands were folded, and he rolled one thumb over the other in a twiddle. It was something she knew he did when he was in deep thought or fought within himself about something that he didn’t want to say.

Finally Lottie said, “I want to ask one question, and I want you to tell me the truth.”

Beck nodded. “That’s fair.”

“That baby Polly had with her...is it yours?” She watched his face.

A flush of red came up from his collar and spread across his face. “No! I didn’t tell you about seeing my children, but I’m a faithful husband...in every way.”

Lottie let out the breath she had held while she waited for his answer.

Chapter 20

June 6, 1903

Annie May and August whispered and giggled in their room. Lottie heard Brody peck on the wall and fuss at the girls.

"Quit your talking and get to sleep. Brody, you and Annie May have to be at work early tomorrow. I have plans for your help, August. The mill doesn't need you, but I do. If the sun comes out and dries up some of the mud, I need you to scrub the dirt off the front porch so we can stop tracking it inside. I don't want to hear no more talk."

The house grew quiet, and nothing else was heard until shortly before midnight. Lottie awoke to heavy rain that had replaced the steady showers from earlier. She had never heard it rain this hard before in her life.

Lottie's foot ached with rheumatism. She lay still and listened to the rain as it beat against the house and prayed that she would dream of happier times. She imagined a day when they would have made enough money to move away from this crowded town. Sleep dulled her thoughts, and the steady drops of rain soothed her back to sleep.

An hour later, Lottie felt a foot push against her ribs. The baby she carried had its nights and days mixed up. It hardly moved during the day but flipped from side to side at night.

Lottie thought of today's date. It was June 6. This was the anniversary of Jacin's death. It was now 1903, and he had died in 1897. Had her baby boy lived, he'd have been six years old. She knew he'd surely be in her thoughts all day. She closed her eyes and remembered his little breaths against her face when she had held him for those few short hours he'd lived. Sleep came, and her dreams faded.

Another heavy downpour woke her at 4:00 a.m. Lottie slipped into the other rooms and shook Annie May and then went to the other room to wake Brody. "Get up and get dressed. I'll have breakfast for you when you come to the kitchen." She planned to rouse Beck at 5:00 and feed him.

The children waited a short time for the trolley, but it failed to come. Lottie stepped out on the porch and watched them slip and slide in the mud as they ran down the hill to their jobs. She could see other young operatives all over the hill doing the same.

The rain beat against the roof and blew in on the porch. Lottie went back into the house to fix August and Beck a bite of breakfast.

***

It was Saturday morning, June 6, 1903 at about a quarter till 6. Beck finished breakfast and waited for the trolley along with John Cantrell and a few other men. It would carry them off the hill and into work.

As with the children earlier that morning, the trolley never arrived. In a few minutes, a crowd of people came running up the tracks. “It’s a flood. Mill Number One is breaking apart and coming down the river. The water has busted through the dams. Everything in its path is washing away.” Everyone tried to talk at once, and Beck listened closely to find out as much as he could about what had happened.

John and the other men decided to hire a carriage and head out to Mill Number One. Beck ran back into the house to tell Lottie.

“The Pacolet is flooding. They say that many of the houses and Mill One has washed away. All through the night, the rain has been like a sheet of water. I can hear a roar in the distance. People are screaming.”

Lottie ran out on the porch and listened. “Brody and Annie May are already at work. What will happen to them? Has anyone checked on the Dexter Mill?”

Lottie yelled back inside to August. “Stay here. If your brother and sister come in, tell them not to leave. I’ll be back as soon as I can.”

Beck pulled Lottie around. "Where do you think you're going? You need to stay inside, what with you in the family way and not long till time to give birth. It's dangerous out there."

Lottie grabbed a hat and pushed it on her head. "I have children that I don't know if they're safe or not. You can't make me stay here, so don't try." Beck stepped out of the way, and Lottie rushed past him.

***

August waited until her Mama and Papa had left in the rain before she went to sit on the porch. People ran in every direction. Some screamed and cried their family's name as they looked for missing people.

Mr. Finley, the next door neighbor ran up the hill. He dragged a young boy of about four years old at his side. Both of them slid down in the yard, and their clothes were muddy. The little boy was sobbing. Mr. Finley crawled up the steps and pulled the boy up beside him.

"Novella,'" he screamed until she ran out on the porch. "Elsie's house has washed away in this flood. Our daughter and the children were sitting on top of it when it broke loose from the foundation and started to float away." He pushed the little boy toward her. "You need to keep him here where it's safe."

Mrs. Finley wrung her hands. "My daughter, oh God, my daughter. What should we do?" She shooed her own baby into the house. "Oh my! Oh my! How did he get off?" She used her apron to wipe his muddy face.

"Elsie and the baby floated away on the house."

"Where was that sorry son-in-law of yours?"

Mr. Finley shook her arm. "Stop it. He tried to save our daughter and their children. He got our grandson out and was swimming back for Elsie and the baby when the house broke loose. It must have hit him in the head. We didn't see him again."

Mrs. Finley bent double and screamed. "We have to find them. I need to come and help."

"You have to stay and watch the boy." He motioned at the crying child. "Two men that tried to help are going down the river, running beside the house to see if they can get to them. I have to run back. If she gets off and swims to safety and then comes here, send someone to get us." He turned to August sitting in a chair. "Send this child. She'll find me." He ran back to the river.

August watched Mrs. Finley moan and cry. She had never liked her but, now, she felt sorry for her.

It was at that minute that August remembered her dream. That woman she'd seen ride by on the house was Elsie. She knew the crying was going to get worse.

Lottie had told her not to leave, but she wanted to see if it looked like it did the night she dreamed about the flood. August slipped off the porch and ran down a ways until she could see the river as it thundered through the mill and the area below the bridge. The sound was loud, but it didn't drown out the cries and screams of the people.

August slipped by three women that huddled together and pointed toward the bend of the river. From her new lookout, she could see people hanging in trees and on top of houses.

She slipped and slid in mud all the way back to the porch. It was just like her dream. August leaned her back against the door of the house and slid down until she sat on the porch. She wrapped her arms around her knees and pushed her face against her muddy legs. *I hope I never have another dream as long as I live. If I have to, I'll never sleep. I'll stay awake the rest of my life!*

***

There was nothing that could have prepared Lottie for what she saw. The water had left its banks and reached outward to the bottom of a cliff above the Dexter Mill. Water was up to near the second floor windows. On the side of the river that she stood, it was up to the rafters on the first row of houses near the river. At the next row of houses, the water reached half way up the front door. People were on top of the roofs screaming for someone to get them. House after house floated down the swollen river, most from Mill Number One.

Lottie gasped as a house passed with only the roof sticking out of the water. On it, a mother and her three children held tight to some rafters exposed by a hole in the top. The mother had the baby in her arms. A boy of about six and a girl of near ten screamed as the house swirled in one direction then twisted and spun the other. They begged for someone to please help them. Dozens of people were on higher grounds above the river but, like her, had no idea what to do. A young man of twelve ran toward the water with the intention of swimming out to the cries of those passing by. His papa grabbed him and explained that the water was too swift, and they would all perish if he tried to do that.

Lottie screamed to men when they run by, "Please help them. We've got to get to the woman and children before they perish." She watched it slam into the limbs of a tree that rushed by them in the swifter water. The tree rolled when it hit the house and a limb knocked the oldest girl into the water and drug her under. She never came to the surface.

An arm came around Lottie's shoulder, and she felt her knees give away.

"That little girl was carried under the water by the tree." Lottie screamed.

Florence sobbed. "I saw it, Lottie." She helped her friend back to her feet. "You need to get inside."

"Annie May and Brody were in the Mill. I need to find if they got out. The water has already filled the inside the mill to the level that Annie May works."

Florence took off the shawl that she had grabbed as she came out the door. She spread it around Lottie's shaking shoulders. "Fate had already gone to work, too. I passed Beck a ways up river. He was yelling at people across the river to see if they had seen my husband or your children. Beck will let us know."

A crash shook another house that floated by. "It must have knocked more trees down upstream. They're coming down the river and hitting everything in their path and taking them under."

Shouts started again near the water. "There are people in those trees on the other side. They're holding on for dear life."

Further down, a man yelled. "There's a girl in a tree down here. Can we get some help?"

Lottie felt her stomach drop. *Is that Annie May's voice I hear*? She tried to run but slipped in the mud and hit the ground.

Florence pulled her up and led her along, going toward the sound of children crying down river.

Brody stood near the edge of the water. Lottie and Florence searched the trees, the water, and the bank on the other side but couldn't find Annie May anywhere.

Brody ran up the hill to where they stood. "I need all the rope, plow lines, sheets, or anything else that's strong enough to hold a body. I'm going to get rope from the well. People are floating down the river. Some are holding onto cotton bales, and some bodies are in trees. It's the worst..."

"There's no time to talk. We see it, too. I'll go with you to get rope." Lottie ran as best she could. She held her bulging belly.

***

Brody and Lottie ran house to house hunting anything that could help pull people from the river.

August was on the porch. "Mama, this is the dream I had. It's all coming true. Please let me come with you."

Lottie looked at August's muddy feet. "August, I told you to stay in the house. Don't come outside. Do you hear me? I'm going back to the river with Brody. Tell your Papa that I'm with Brody."

"But my dream, Mama!"

"I know. It came true. We'll talk about this later, but now I need to know you're safe in the house.

"Yes ma'am." August stood by the door and peeped out. "I didn't die in the dream," she yelled.

Lottie stopped and looked back at August. *Do I dare ask who did? No time now.*

Lottie grabbed the plow lines from a nail under the steps . "Brody, take down the clothes line out back and get the well rope. It's lying at the mouth of the well. Bring both with you. The clothes line might not hold a body, but it might help tie something."

Darker clouds blew overhead and spilled buckets more of rain. Lottie grabbed her soaked dress, twisted the tail of it between her hands, and squeezed out the heavy water as she ran. If Lottie lived to be a hundred, she'd never forget what she had seen and heard.

She ran back to the water. She couldn't find Brody.

The levels were higher than before. The water circled and pushed against a house that earlier had very little water around it. The whole family had climbed on the roof. They screamed and begged for someone to help. Below them, a woman and baby clung to the top of a bale of cotton as it rushed by. The mother clung to the wire that held it together with one hand and squeezed her arm about her baby with the other. The bundle of cotton was attached to a rope held by four men on the other side of the river. Lottie stopped and saw the rope go tight with a jerk. When it did, the woman grabbed tighter to the ties on the bale to hold on, but she dropped her baby over the side. She screamed as the child was carried away by the rushing water.

Florence rushed up to Lottie. She grabbed her hand and pulled her nearer to the water's edge. "Look over there on the other side, over where the store used to stand. Mr. Stribling is in that tree. They said he was plum naked until a woman on that other limb above him let him have her apron to cover up his private parts. Nobody's been able to get to either one of them."

"Surely some of those people over there can do something." Lottie wrung her hands.

Florence put her arm around Lottie's shoulder, and they sobbed. Lottie pulled out a wet hanky from her bosom and blew her nose. "They say the water is about forty feet higher than usual, and some say it's running forty miles an hour. That's too swift to help anyone."

Lottie fought her way through the crowds that screamed in sorrow as they watched friends and family pulled away from the banks of the water. They were too shocked to help. Not that there was much anyone could do once you were dragged into the rushing water.

Florence slid down and grabbed Lottie's dress tail. "There's Lizzie in that tree. She's right there." She pointed at a tree below where a foot log had once been.

Lottie saw the fear on Lizzie's face. "Oh God help us. Annie May and Lizzie were together in the mill. Help me find Annie May." Lottie's eyes searched the water for her daughter.

She ran closer to the edge. A hand reached out from the crowd that had gathered to watch. It was Annie May. Lottie grabbed her. She cried as she wiped mud from her daughter's face.

Annie May pushed her mother's hand away. "We have to help Lizzie. I tried to get others to help, but everyone has a person they're trying to help already, or else they're too scared. Please, we can't let her die." Tears streaked down the red mud smear on her face. She turned and pushed through the crowd. She ran toward Lizzie.

Lottie screamed. “Annie May, come back up here. Don’t get close to the water. If you slip and fall, it’ll pull you under.”

When Lottie got to her, she had torn the plow reins out of Brody’s hands and tied them together. She threw them at her friend. Lizzie failed to catch it, and Annie May tried again. This time Lizzie grabbed hold. She jumped from the tree, hoping Annie May could pull her to the side.

“Wait....wait until you tie it around you,” Lottie screamed. The words were too late. The swift waters jerked her body downstream and took Annie May with her.

Lottie ran down the edge and watched the water pull the two girls along. Once Annie May caught hold of a tree, but lost her hold when Lizzie pulled hard on the rope. Annie May tried to tie the rope around her own waist. “Let go of the rope, child. You can’t save her. She’ll drown you and herself.”

“Mama, I can’t let go of her. I can’t. She’s my best friend,” she screamed.

“You have to. Please. Grab hold to the next tree, and let go of her.”

“No!” She choked on the water that rushed into her open mouth.

Lottie looked up and saw the entire building coming toward the girls. It was the Presbyterian Church that had stood on the Eastern side of the River in the bend below Mill Two. The edge of the church clipped the tree and slammed into both Annie May and Lizzie. That was the last time Lottie saw either of them.

***

Brody found Lottie at the place where she had last seen the girls. She rocked back and forth and was covered from head to foot in mud.

"Mama, come with me. Papa is pulling people to the side. You can help."

Lottie looked at Brody. "Annie May went under and so did Lizzie. They both perished. They didn't come up after the church hit them. Why didn't Beck come and help me save her? She's the one that needed saving."

"What? We didn't know Annie May was seen in the water." Brody ran to a pile of lumber wedged against a tree. There was no sign of life. "Are you sure she went under? Maybe she rode some part of the house on down …."

Lottie put both hands over her ears and screamed. "No. It was not that pile of lumber that hit her. It was the Church as it floated by."

"But she might have caught hold here…" The roar of the river and screams drowned out his words, as he forgot about his Papa and ran down the riverside looking for signs of Annie May.

Upstream about two hundred feet, Lottie heard a voice yell. "Please, someone help me. I'm here. Don't go away. Help me." She heard babies crying.

She saw children, men, and women desperately hugging house tops, cotton bales, trees, and anything that would float.

She looked up the hill above her at a long line of people watching. They were too afraid to come near the water.

She turned to run downstream with Brody. Her feet tripped on a woman lying with her body half in the water and half on the sand. At the woman's waist lay a young boy of about three or four.

Across the woman's chest was a baby that was probably a few months old. The rushing water pushed them closer to Lottie's feet. The woman's gown had washed up around her neck. The baby that lay across her bare body was completely naked. The little boy at her feet also had no clothes. The bodies had not been there moments ago.

Lottie stooped, fell down on her hands and knees, and threw up. She wiped her mouth.

Two men came to where she was. "That's Oliver and Novella Finley's daughter and her baby. The little boy is not theirs. I'm not sure who he belongs to."

Lottie looked at the body again. She reached over and raked back the mud and weeds that covered the young woman's face. They were right. She swallowed the puke that came up again in her mouth. She crawled to a bush and pulled herself up, and followed Brody down the river.

“Mama, there’s a girl in a tree down there past the curve at Santuc. She’s just a little ways out.” Brody pointed down the river.

She grabbed his hand, and they ran together. Lottie tripped, and Brody helped her back up.

“It’s not her. Annie had on a green shirt. That girl’s top is blue.”

They watched the water rise higher on the young girl. It came over her feet and rose quickly to her waist. She tried to climb to the next limb. “Help me. Please help me.” She screamed as a snake ran over her hand. Just above her were a squirrel and two raccoons that had climbed to get away from the water. Two other snakes dangled from a limb above her head.

Lottie shivered. “We can’t help her. We have to look for Annie.”

Brody looked to the people over the hillside. He yelled at a group of men coming toward them with ropes in their hand. He pointed, “That girl needs help.”

The men rushed a hundred feet up-river from the girl. They pulled a bale of cotton away from a tree, tied the rope to the bale binding, and put a man on it. They pushed him out and let the stream carry him to the tree with the girl. She was saved.

Lottie and Brody ran down the river side, screaming Annie May’s name.

***

Beck met Lottie and Brody walking back up the bank of the river. Brody had his arm around his mother.

"We couldn't find Annie May. She's gone." Lottie fell into Beck's arms, limp and eyes closed. He picked her up and carried her.

"I just found out she was in the water, or I would have come sooner."

Beck looked down at Brody.

Tears ran down his face. He wiped his nose with his muddy shirt sleeve. "Papa, there was a whole family on top of a house at the dam. The man grabbed a tree as they went over the dam, and he got to the side of the river. But, we watched his wife and three kids go over it. We sat there for quite a spell hoping to get sight of Annie May. A man passed us coming up river that said he watched that man's wife and children float at least three miles down."

Beck stopped and adjusted Lottie's body to make her easier to carry. "It's terrible…the damage and lives lost. I have to get your Mama to the house. I hope she don't lose this baby she's carrying. She's going to need it to keep her mind off all her sorrow, if that's possible, anyways."

Lottie opened her eyes. "I hear you talking about me, Beck. I'd gladly give this baby I've not seen to save the one I already have." She cried. "My sweet Annie May. I fear she's gone for good." Lottie's eyes closed and her head and body became lifeless when she passed out from exhaustion.

***

Beck stayed with Lottie until she slept then went back to the river. It had been eight hours since the first buildings at the upper mill had been swept away. People still held tightly to tree limbs, their strength almost gone.

A group of men placed two cotton bales together and tied them to a rope they had wrapped around a tree. Beck and three others let the rope out gently while one man rode it out to where a woman and her two children had climbed to the highest limbs of a tree that had pushed itself against some rocks. In the tree beside them was a man, S.B. Johnson, who had been borne upon the raging waters for two miles before he grabbed hold and climbed in beside them. He cried as they pulled him back to the shore. He fell on the ground and rolled to his back. "I fear my wife and five children have drowned. One son might have made it. I saw him float away holding tightly to a piece of timber.

The Reverend in the group shook his head to the others, and tried to whisper. "Someone told me they saw him go over the dam at Pacolet and disappear in the fifteen foot waves that covered the dam and shoals."

Mr. Johnson looked up. "I figured as much." He turned away from them, and his body shook.

***

Beck left Lottie on the bed with her face to the wall. She wouldn't speak, and her shoulders shook as she cried. Nothing would comfort her. August had climbed up beside her and curled up at her back and slept.

He needed to see if anyone else had seen Annie May and Lizzie. It was noon, and the water levels had dropped considerably. There were still people hanging onto lumber or cotton bales in the middle of the river, yelling for a rescue. More cotton bales lay on the banks and others floated near the edge. Lumber and parts of houses were wedged against trees with arms or legs sticking out between them. People pulled at the boards to find out if it was someone they knew. Word spread that there were hundreds of people missing.

Lizzie's Papa walked toward Beck with a body wrapped in material from a bolt from one of the mills that he had found near the water's edge. Beck ran to help.

"It's my Lizzie. She was stuck between a cotton bale and a tree when the waters receded. Annie May was not there. I'm sorry."

Beck watched the water drip from the bundle. The material was from the mill that he worked. He remembered when they made it. It was so pretty. He had wished he could afford some of it to let Lottie make a dress for her and the girls.

Beck walked behind the man as he carried his daughter up the hill and to their home. Beck stopped and sat down on the porch when they passed his and Lottie's house. He put his head between his knees. This had once been a peaceful valley. He had brought his family here in hopes of making enough money to get ahead in life. He wanted to be able to afford to buy clothes and shoes for his children. Instead he had lost three children...two to the fever and it now looked like one to this flood. Lottie's dream had come to pass. Why hadn't be believed her and left when she knew this was the place? He couldn't blame Lottie if she hated him. He wouldn't have done this for any amount of money in the world, if he had known.

Chapter 21

June 1903

The sight of Annie May's body wrapped in a dirty sheet would never leave Lottie's memory as long as she lived. Someone came upon her Annie about a mile downstream covered in sand. They had noticed her hand sticking through the gravel, dug her out, and brought her to the bottom of the hill near where the bridge to the mill had been. Lottie had run away when Beck took her in his arms. She had walked up the river, and fell on her knees in the middle of the road.

Most all bodies that could be found had been and were carried home and burials planned for the next day.

The water was almost back to normal, and people sifted through sand and gravel and looked for belongings. One man dug near where his house had been and pulled out box springs. He sat on the edge of the water and picked out the sand. He carried water and poured it over them until they were clean.

"There are a right smart of piled bed springs further down the river. It'd be easier to get one of those."

He looked up at her and nodded. "I know, but this one was the springs my wife and I set up housekeeping with." He reached in his pocket and pulled out a hairpin and a muddy purse he had found trapped in the springs. "She wore this hairpin, and this was the purse she carried to church."

Lottie nodded and moved on. She left him in tears as he held the purse near his heart.

She saw women pick up several bolts of cloth from a pile and carry them home. Lottie dug in the pile. It was at the bottom that she saw the material that Annie May had talked about when they had spun it a week ago. She had loved that material. She talked about how it would make the most beautiful dress. Lottie grabbed it and ran toward the house.

***

Brody helped Beck make the casket as he had with Tolliver. They fetched the lumber they had hauled up from the river bank. Beck measured. Brody sawed.

Lottie heated water and lovingly washed her eldest daughters muddy body. She washed her from the neck down and covered her with a quilt. Lottie got fresh water and a new cloth to wash her face and hair. “You were the sweetest baby girl. Brody cried the first three months after he was born, but you were as good as gold. Never gave me a minute’s trouble. I wish I had told you more how much I loved you.”

Brody stood in the door. “She knew it Mama. She loved you, too.”

Lottie shook her head and continued to comb Annie May’s hair. Tears ran down her face.

Beck slipped in beside Brody. “I have it ready. Let me have her.”

“Stop. I have some material. I’m going to make her a dress to wear. She loved this material.” Lottie grabbed the bolt of material for Beck to see.

“No. You can’t use that material. It’s not yours.”

“Everybody is taking some. It ain’t no good for the mill to sell. It’s ruined. I can wash it and make her a pretty dress.”

“You take that material back down there and leave it where you found it. Take it right now.”

Lottie looked at him like he was a stranger. “What are you talking about? They don’t want this material. It ain’t stealing. Even if it was, I don’t care. I want to make Annie May a dress.”

“Take it back.” Beck picked up Annie May and took her outside. He laid her into the casket still wrapped in the quilt. He hammered the top on the box. He picked her up and took her into the house.

Lottie screamed at him. “It ain’t no different than you going down there and picking up that there lumber from the piles of stuff that washed down in the flood and you using it to make Annie May's casket."

Beck came back and looked at her. They stared at each other without saying a word.

Lottie sat down on the steps of the porch and wept.

When she got up, she ran to the river. She slung the material as far as she could throw it into the middle of the water, turned, and walked slowly back to the house.

***

Later that afternoon, Beck dug a grave beside Sheffield and Tolliver.

Lottie sat by Annie May. It was not much use trying to have a funeral as almost everybody had a family member or friend that had perished. There was not enough time to take them one at a time to have a burial.

While Beck was at the cemetery digging, there had been six others placing their loved ones in the ground. Two others were also digging graves.

Lottie and August walked down by the river. Three men walked on the sand banks.

"Did you lose everything?" Lottie asked.

"I've came upon some of our possessions, but that does not compare to losing my family."

Lottie nodded and swallowed to keep from sobbing. "My husband is digging our daughter's grave."

One of the two men with him said, "We've not found the bodies of his family, yet. We were told that if you watched for a crack in the sand and, if flies are flying near it, to dig. There's probably a body there."

Lottie's hand flew to her mouth, and her eyes filled with tears. "I can't stand it here any longer."

The man looked at the swarm of flies at a crack in the sand below him and said, "I can't leave. My family will be here forever. How can I leave them?"

Another man said, "The river gave us life's needs when we had nothing but the clothes on our back, and now it has taken life away. The Lord gives, and the Lord takes away is all we can say."

***

Sleep came to none of them that night. They took turns sitting by Annie May while the others packed the crates with their belongings. The last of their possessions was tied on the wagon.

Novella watched out the window as they packed the wagon. Lottie walked over to the window where she sat and motioned for her to come outside.

"I'm sorry about your daughter, son-in-law, and grandbaby. It's a dark time in your life, and I'm sorry. I'm sorry for any unhappiness me or my family may have caused. We're moving on to find work. There ain't room for one of our beds, and I left it there in the bedroom. I know you have your other grandson to raise, so you are welcome to that bed if you want it.

Novella swallowed hard and nodded. She didn't speak, and tears fell onto her bosom. Lottie reached out and hugged her then went to the wagon.

Beck pushed in a shovel beside a few other hand tools he had packed on the wagon earlier. "I've finished loading, and I'm ready to go up to the graveyard." He picked up the casket and put it across the back of the wagon. "Brody, sit on the edge and don't let her fall off." He motioned for August to get in the middle of the seat, and then he helped Lottie on the wagon.

At the graveyard, Beck and Brody carried Annie May, and Lottie and August walked behind. They put the casket into the hole. Lottie sat on the ground between the other two graves and watched them cover it. August sat beside her and cried.

They packed the dirt with their feet, and Beck put a field rock at the head of the grave.

"You promised me that we'd get real markers."

Beck stared at her.

Lottie frowned. "You promised. If we don't put markers on there, nobody will know who's lying here."

Beck handed the shovel to Brody. "Put it back on the wagon." He turned back to Lottie. "It don't matter if they know or not. We know where they are, and they ain't here. Their bodies will return to dust."

"You can be a mean man, Beck. I know they ain't, but I left them here. This was the last place their body laid. My family marks our graves." Lottie cried.

Beck shoved his hair back with his hand. "We'll come back someday and put tombstones when we can afford to buy 'em."

"I never said we had to have real costly ones. It would've been fine if you chiseled their name and date of birth and death on it yourself. If you notched deep enough, it'd last for years and years. What if we come back and can't find their graves?"

"We can find them. I buried them. I'll know where they are. I couldn't forget."

Brody helped August into the wagon then went to sit on the back where the casket had been.

"Get on, and let's go." Beck helped Lottie up.

She waited until he came around and sat down beside her. "Why do we have to leave? Others are staying for a few days. We'd still have time for you to do the headstones if we wait another day or two."

"You realize there are hundreds here without a job. We have to get ahead of everyone and get to another mill. We need to get the jobs before they're gone."

"Just one day. Please. Make headstones."

Beck's face reddened. "Lottie, you're going to have a baby soon. We have two other children. We have to feed them. To do that, I have to have a job.

If we don't outrun the others, we may not get work. The train to Morganton leaves this afternoon, and we need to be on it when it pulls out."

"I hate you, right now, Beck Radford. I told you when we came that this was a place of sorrow. It's proved to be everything I said. When are you going to listen to me when I tell you my dreams almost always come true? I am sick of the sorrow."

Beck said, "There's something else you need to think about. After all this rain, the sickness may return. Our family has dwindled down, and I don't want to lose another one of you. People have talked about other places that had a flood like this and, soon after, the fever raged. I'll listen to you next time. I've learned my lesson well."

Chapter 22

June 1903

The train belched out black smoke. Beck leaned toward Lottie and pulled her head on his shoulder to rest. Around them were other families, some they knew from Clifton and from other mills that had been destroyed by the flood. One or two men slept, along with a few children. One man stared out the window and had never looked anywhere else for the past half hour. Beck could see the side of his face. The only movement the man had made was to wipe tears that Beck saw run down his cheek.

Lottie stirred and Beck pulled her head down into his lap. Her hair was damp and curled around her face. Brody and August sat on the seat in front of them. They gladly let South Carolina disappear from the back of the train. The gentle hills of North

Carolina took some of the people's mind off the move.

Beck and Lottie had come as a family of six, and even though Tolliver had been borne to them in Clifton making seven, they were leaving as a family of four.

Beck had laid his hand over Lottie, and it rested on her stomach. Beneath the palm of his hand, there was a hard kick. Soon there would be five of them, if the Lord willed.

He drew a deep breath and thought about the last three years. Hope was an odd thing. It could bloom in the desert of the heart of man even when everything around him was dead and bleak. People were made to be tough and strong. Man appeared to find a way to dig out of hopelessness and hunt new fields to plow and a place to plant their dreams, all in faith of better times. There were some that wallowed like a pig in their pain. He knew he couldn't judge them, but it was a waste of life. There was nothing you can change about the past. But the future was a story yet to be written.

With one heart ache after another in the past three years, Beck had to admit there were times he would have liked to have left it behind him, like he had once before.

Sheffield, Tolliver, and Annie May, he had left deep in the ground on Vinegar Hill. He had also left behind his other children for the second time. Peter was a man and understood more than Billy, Sarah, or Maude. Thank God, the mill where Peter worked had assured him he would be used in their rebuilding. It gave Beck peace to know that his son had a job. It would see he had the necessities of life.

Lottie sat up. “Are we there yet?”

Beck laughed. “You sound like a child. No, we’re not there, but it won’t be long.”

She laid her head backward against his arm that he had curled along the back of their seat. “Will we live in one of those two-family houses like we did in Clifton?”

“I don’t know, but I reckon they’re all alike.” Beck rubbed Lottie’s head. “Lottie, I want you to know that we’re going to get a home and farm of our own someday. It won’t take much longer until there will be enough money to show that we’re in earnest about buying a place. Me and Brody will go right to work. August is ten years old, and it won’t take long until they hire her. With all three of us working, the bank will give us a loan. Somebody told me we wouldn’t have to pay all the money up front.”

The train jostled to a stop at the last town before they reached their destination. The children were both asleep, August’s head in Brody’s lap.

Lottie stared at the children and said softly to Beck. “I know we’ll make it, by the grace of God. I figure it can’t get worse than this. It has to get better, right?”

“I’ve made many promises to you. Up until now, it probably don’t seem like I’ll keep any. But, I’ll do my best to fulfill all of them, if I can. Life will be more tolerable as soon as we're working. Keep the faith. I intend that this family will prosper."

Lottie smiled. "I do trust you. You keep the faith too."

Beck pulled her toward him and kissed the top of her head. "I believe we'll be moving to Tennessee in three to five years at the most. That'll be our brand new start. Until then, we work extra hard."

Lottie fell back to sleep as soon as the train pulled out of the station, carried in her dreams back to her Papa, Mama, and her beloved mountains.

The End